I0534314

The Blending of the Realms

*Lifting the veil of uncertainty to have
all remember what they have forgotten.
It is time.*

Written

By DB Lorgan

Copyright © 2020 DBLorgan

All rights reserved.

ISBN-13: 978-0-9861097-4-4

ISBN-10: 0-9861097-4-6

By DB Lorgan.

All rights are reserved. No part of this book may be used or reproduced, stored in or introduced into a retrieval system, or transmitted in any form or by any means without the express written consent of the author of this book

Further inquiries can be addressed to:

DBLorgan Productions

dblorgan@hotmail.com

Perry, New York 14530

Published and printed in the
United States of America
Religion / Spirituality
New Age/ Spirituality
Angels/ Spirit Guides

Enjoy the playful and intriguing way DBLorgan creates her characters to surround you with excitement and anticipation in each of her novels.

You will see that they are like none others that you have ever read as you read them.

This little book is sure to touch your heart, allowing you to see life with a clearer view than you ever thought possible.

She will help you learn how to manifest your desires so that you shall be living the joyous and fulfilling life you deserve.

Her works include:

The Memory Barrel: 2009

The Memory Barrel ~ Second Edition: 2015

In the Eyes of the Beholder: 2018

My wish for you:

Forever Mom and Dad

Letter from the Author:

They say that experience is the best teacher. Sitting here, I'm beginning to understand that more and more. My last novel, In the Eye of the Beholder, was released in 2019.
It took me five years to write In the Eye of the Beholder and seven years to write The Memory Barrel.

Today, I have been given my next novel by my angels: The Blending of the Realms: I will proceed and let it flow as the others have.

Throughout the years, I have been a student on so many different levels. Some were joyful, and some not so much. I have been a writer, an observer of life most of my world to share what I have seen and experienced. Not to give an opinion about things, but to allow the reader to do that within themselves.

This novel will take you personally into many unique experiences. A task few authors dare to take on. Yet, I do feel it is possible. Possible so the experiences that stir your soul will calm it from within.

For you to experience "The Blending of the Realms", hold the book and open your heart to an understanding you had before coming to the realm of time.

The spiritual realm and the realm of time co-exist simultaneously.

Let's begin side by side if you're ready, then turn the next page

DBLorgan

I dedicate this book to

YOU--

May you be enlightened and inspired by my novels.

Namaste

Chapter One

The last year in this little town, many experienced a unique connection with the ethereal realm. Given direction and told of an experience that was going to take place in the earthly. -
Who were the messengers of this unbelievable task?
Who would be chosen to guide this along?
Would the angels come and create it? Or would human beings be used to make the unbelievable believable?
As you continue to read, you will understand, walking side by side with the enlightened and others becoming enlightened to truly experience a blending of the realms, making the unbelievable believable.

The hidden village of Saol was changing. They knew it would happen. All the villagers were very aware; time was going to change. Just as the seasons change, so will this little village. Life goes on, and Saol was to be available for all to enjoy.

The people here were the threads that made this town magical and welcoming. The visitors were plentiful now, coming from all over the world. Curious to see the lake named after dreams. The village and lake seemed to possess magic in the very fabric of their existence. The presentation worldwide of the documentary about Talise Kavanaugh: "The Beholder" brought this little village to view. It was her home. I think they are trying to find the magic Talise talked of in her documentary. Time will tell if they can be touched by it as she was. Time will tell.

Old and young were gathering today to pay their respects to Talise, who touched hearts worldwide for years.

Today is her day of celebration of life since she journeyed to Spirit with her friend Vivian. Yes, they walked into their next chapter together — side by side.

~*~

The little restaurant called The Journey on Main Street was filled. People were waiting outside just to enjoy the ambiance they had read about.

Laura came back to the kitchen. Her boyfriend, Tim O'Farrell, was with her. Everyone was so busy creating their unique recipes. "Maggie, can we help?"

"Ahh, love, your creativity is for the world to see on your television station. Not here in the kitchen. Go out there and see what words you can share. Timothy take care of her," she said with a motherly voice.

Laura smiled. "Alright, where is Brenna?"

I think she is making the final arrangements for our celebration. Is Joseph with you? I have some of his special pie set aside for him."

"He's down at the Haven. He'll be here in a few minutes. He mentioned the pie this morning. I think he's just gathering his thoughts. I know it's hard. I heard him crying last night in his room."

"Tears are the cleansing of the soul; it will be alright. He'll be alright; it takes time for the storm of sadness to pass."

~*~

Joe walked this path by the lake a few months ago with Laura's mother, Vivian. He felt a connection with her and Talise. Similar to what he had with his mother and grandmother.

"I know everything will be alright." he thought. He sat down on the old Adirondack chair by the water. He heard footsteps coming up behind him.

A sweet Gaelic voice said. "Would ya like some company?"

He smiled, "Hi, Brenna, company is what I do need."

"I thought so. I was driving by and saw your car still here. Laura must be in town then?"

"She was up at the crack of dawn today. I'm not sure if that girl sleeps." He sighed with concern.

She nuzzled next to him, "do you mind? I need to be close to someone."

He put his arm around her; they both seemed to be numb as they watched the water flowing in and out. The silence calmed them both.

"Are you ready for today?"

"I think so. I found a note mom wrote on her bedside table for this."

"Really? Are you alright with sharing it?

"Yes, I hope she gives me some of her strength to get through it without breaking down into tears."

Joe pulled her closer, "take some from me."

He remembered the words her mother Talise had shared so often.

This made her smile.

They drove into town together.

The sight of cars lined up on both sides of the road surprised them.

Joe smiled, noticing one parking place right in front of The Journey, as he pulled in. They both laughed and said, "Thank you, Mom!"

They entered the little café; no sooner as they closed the door, a motherly voice called out.

"There ya be! I've been waitin for ya' both. Ya' better be hungry!"

Joe gave Maggie a huge hug. She pulled Brenna close to her too.

"Your pie is being kept warm in the kitchen," she whispered in his ear.

Joe snickered, "By the fairies, I'm guessing."

She ruffled his hair, "But, of course!"

He felt like he was home. He had a family again.

Laura came up behind Brenna, "Hello, love."

Brenna turned and hugged her.

~*~

The café filled and emptied and then filled again. Everyone was there to celebrate Talise Kavanaugh, "The Beholder." Food was plentiful and laughter, along with live music serenading everyone in attendance.

A sweet young girl was singing an ancient Gaelic song as the violin and guitar strummed nearby. "A ghaoil, leig dhachaigh gum mhàthair mi": Brenna stood beside the girl and sang the song with her. Her voice was like a soft angelic melody.

Outside, you could hear the bagpipes playing, serenading the love of all in the realm of time and the realm of spirit for these two lovely ladies who have begun their journey in the realm of no time.

Brenna walked outside, singing with the band behind her. Her voice carried up the village path. It echoed as if carried by the wind to cover the mountainous canyon that this little village was nestled within.

Everyone within the café came outside on the walkway.

The music continued; Brenna took hold of Laura's hand, guiding her toward the old oak tree in the town garden.

Brenna began:

"Welcome, to all family and friends on this day of celebration for two beautiful souls. My mother Talise has never ceased to amaze me and proved it again this morning. She was sensing my hesitation to address all of you today. She was the speaker in the family. Now she has passed her gift to me, it seems. My songs were only shared in private; now, her love has given me the confidence to sing to you from my heart. Blessings to you all.

"On my bed stand, a letter rested for me this morning. It just appeared because it wasn't there last night. She left it for me to share with you."

She read her mother's letter:

While I was present in this realm, I came to teach you and others to believe in themselves, to trust in yourself. There are so many innumerable ways to teach that are far above your ways of thinking. In the ethereal realm, there are great masters, angels in all statures and essence. Spirit beings, though many of you haven't been taught these things, they do exist. I know this may seem complicated, but it all comes down to you.

What are your thoughts? Do they give you peace or fear? Is the fear of what you are being shown contrary to what you were taught? Does this make it unacceptable and "evil" if others feel this is their path of life, and it brings them joy?

Consider and realize our infinite universe exists within an infinite creator, to whether your concept is a male or female. Since indeed, the infinite is both. Since how can anything come to be if it was not of the infinite? It can- not.

We all in the realm of time and the ethereal life, move and have our very being within the Infinite Spirit-- Your books of worship confirm this exact statement.

Look at life as a buffet. You, of course, can't consume the entire buffet at one time. Make your selections in life by visual and by all your senses. You possess these senses for your well-being. Take a little here, if that doesn't agree with you. You set it aside. Please, please don't discourage anyone else from trying it since it might be pleasing to them. Do you see?

All have the right to choose. Now, remember this: All have the right to choose.
Abundant life filled with joy, Is what I wish for you.
Talise Kavanaugh.

The people were silent, considering what was just shared.

Laura stepped forward:
"Hello, everyone, and welcome. Allow me to introduce myself. I am Laura Lang, you know me as the producer of the documentary, The Beholder. I realized after a short time with Talise, my family and hers were connected.

"They are connected through a sisterhood of the heart, beginning with Brenna's great-great-grandmother.

"I have learned from Talise many things; I had no way of knowing before I met her. Through her writings, she will continue to guide and teach us all.

"Remember, you are never alone. Your spiritual family encompasses your life and your children's life. It is a never-ending relationship that is now for you to be aware of and make those that aren't also aware.

"Brenna and I will continue our journey as sisters of the heart as our mothers were and still are.

"We are all of the same family here, just as it is in Spirit. Today is a day of joy for us all. Let's continue Talise and Vivian's celebration of life with fun and laughter. Your and my life never ends; we continue to the spirit realm to another chapter and continue living. If someone has taught you differently, I say show them a seed or a butterfly: changes don't mean death or an ending. It is a beginning for us all.

"My sister" ---- (she touched Brenna's hand) "We wish you joy. Now let's have some fun, okay?"

Everyone cheered. "Okay"

Chapter Two

Laura's words flowed through her pencil to the paper in front of her:

She knew full well what was taking place. The book she had been given at the Haven in Saol sat on her desk beside her tablet. The book that answered all questions, she was told.

A knock at the door took Laura's attention from her writing.

"Hey there!" She said, surprised to see Joe, her co-worker.

Laura and Joe worked at a local television station in Boston. They had been side by side for years, creating some very engaging documentaries worldwide. She was now the assistant producer of the entire station. Life had changed for her.

"It looks like I arrived just in the nick of time! I can tell you're up to something."

"Yes, you were always able to read me. I'm having a hard time trying to put everything together. I'm not sure what I'm doing next."

"I can see your tense; let's pour you a glass of wine, lass," he revealed a bottle hidden behind his back.

Laura pulled him inside, grabbing his empty arm, "You know I can never turn away a bearer of gifts."

He poured the wine, "So what are you up to?" He could see papers scattered everywhere around her desk and all over the floor.

"I'm writing *a book....*" She was silent, waiting for his response.

Then looked over at all the papers, she quickly took another long gulp.

"Are you ready to do it?"

"When is anyone ever truly ready? It has to start somewhere. This morning just seemed to be the day."

"Wow, this is going to be exciting. If you need a co-author, just say so."

"You mean co-conspirator, don't you?" Laura teased.

"You always have co-conspired with me on everything. Trust me; I will be calling you! Maybe at the most inconvenient times!

My friend, you barely had time to unpack from the trip. And you're jumping right into this now. Are you sure?"

"I have to. I'll explode if I don't."

"How's your new buddy doing?"

"Hey, boy," rustling Shadow's hair. "This is a temporary change, my friend. We will be returning to Saol soon. I promise."

She brought him home with her, not by her choice by his. He jumped into her car while packing to return to Boston and nestled in the back seat. He was now her companion.

~*~

Joe curled up in the corner chair, watching Laura. His thoughts, remembering back to their travels at Lake Aisling. He knew she was keeping busy trying not to think of what happened. He was worried. *"I'll just keep my eyes on her,"* he thought. *"We'll be fine."*

Looking around the room, he remembered the last time he had been sitting there; everyone was viewing The Beholder, the documentary Laura and he had put together. The documentary was well-received worldwide. Sharing a story of an awe-inspiring woman Talise Kavanaugh. The Beholder.

The night they wished never happened.

Joe began remembering:

The phone rang:

Joe answered, "Yes, she's right here."

Laura came out of the kitchen, and their eyes met.

"It's Brenna," he said.

The look on her face required no words as Brenna shared the passing of her mother and Laura's mom.

We had learned so much with our time spent in this little town of Saol.

Laura repeated to him and Tim what took place:

"Mom and Vivian put on their coats so excited to go out in the darkness by the water. Brenna called to them to stop because it was so dark, she could barely make out where they were. The moon's reflection on the water created a mist floating above it. There was an uneasiness within her.

"They were so quick," Brenna cried. "I asked them to wait for me. I wanted to go with them.

"My mom laughed and said, 'You're always with us, angel.'

"They ran out the door like two young girls playing in the night. What was strange is that Shadow just lay there in his bed, not moving a muscle, sound asleep. He always followed Talise wherever she went.

"Brenna leaned on the porch beam, watching them dancing around in the night, laughing and singing. Then they giggled and dropped to the bench. Still chattering away---

"She called out to them, "Okay, you two, it is way past your bedtime. Do you want me to bring you some tea?"

"Both their hands raised, acknowledging they heard her. She had to be careful walking down the path because the light seemed to have dulled a bit. When she reached the bench, they both were so quiet. They were holding hands."

Laura's voice vibrated, telling them. "They went together. Our mothers went together!"

The tears flowed down Laura's face. She dropped to the floor sobbing.

Joe lay on the floor beside her holding her. Tim was sitting next to her, holding his head in disbelief.

~*~

"Joe!" Laura yelled. "Look at this. I'm sure this is what was meant when we were at the Haven. Oh my god!"

He had dozed off and jumped to a stand from the chair, being startled by her yelling.

"My god, Laura, you scared the crap out of me!"

"Oh, I'm sorry I didn't know you were sleeping. Come on. There is no time to sleep."

"Do we stay in this realm? Because you just nearly caused my heart to stop. You can't do that to me. I'm getting too old for this stuff!"

She snickered, "Yes, of course, silly! I'm not Talise and can't do what she did, yet it's the next best thing!"

"Do we need or have a budget to finance this thing?"

"I think I can get all the help we need."

Joe smiled, "Of course you can. I do not doubt that."

"Come on, let's get away from the city!" She grabbed her notes and slid them in her briefcase."

"Oh, you mean the world of concrete?" He teased her.

"Exactly, oh my gosh, we have to go see Brenna! Go home and get packed. I'll call you in the morning.

~

Talise and Vivian did a happy dance.

"She's still in tune with us, Viv. This is going to be enlightening for her and her true awakening.

With this, anything is possible."

"Who do you have in mind to visit her?" Vivian asked.

"We shall see. She will have many visitors in the upcoming months."

"Laura, my god, what time is it?" Joe looked at the clock on his phone. "Seven o'clock in the morning, are you kidding me? It's Sunday."

She ignored his whining and continued.

"Is she planning to return to Ireland?"

"I'm not sure," he answered.

"I'll give her a quick call." Laura was insisting on knowing the answer at this very moment.

"May I suggest letting her wake up before you do!"

She hesitated...

"Are you still there, were we disconnected?" He *whispered*, "I hope so, maybe I can sleep--"

"NO!" She shouted. "I am not disconnected. And I heard that!"

He started laughing, and she joined in.

"You're not disconnected, aye.? I beg to differ."

"Funny, you're just so funny, Joseph. Maybe you should see if you can join comedy central. Then when you are, I can TURN YOU OFF!!"

She softened her voice with a girly whine to it. "Meet me in an hour at the coffee shop?

He laughed; he knew what she was doing. "I'll be there."

~*~

Brenna's phone rang. It took her longer to answer than she expected. A faint voice said. "Yah' better not be messing with me," in her Gaelic accent.

Laura laughed. "Hi Brenn, are you okay?"

"Ohhh," --- she cleared her voice. "Yes, yes. Hi, Laura, I'm fine. I thought you were another one of the telemarketers. My god, how do you handle this constant ringing and texting from them?"

"I just hang up, or if I don't recognize the number, I let it ring. If it's important, they will leave a message."

"The more it happens, the more I realize why mum would have nothin' to do with them."

"Are you up for some more company Brenna?"

"Sure, when were you thinking?"

"I'm going to check with the cabin mom rented last year. To see if I can come there for a week. I know it's a long time, but I'm having some difficulty getting into the swing of things around here. Plus, who knows, we might need a large gathering location again."

"Is your job alright?"

"Yes, that's fine. Tom has lightened my load. I know you're returning to Ireland soon, and I wanted to spend some time with you before you go. If that's okay."

"Of course, it is. Let me know when you're arriving." They were about to hang up.

"Laura?"

"Yes."

"Is Joe coming too?"

"You couldn't hold him back even if I wanted to. Tim is coming too, and don't forget Shadow."

Brenna laughed. "Okay, then see you soon."

Chapter Three

In the ethereal realm, a gathering of the enlightened elders and guides was taking place.

Gabriel led the discussion.

"Now, it is time to make our presence more palpable in the world of time.

"It seems we are only sharing this information with a few specific inhabitants in the realm of time, yet there are thousands more that are learning the same thing. The same revelation of this experience. Is being shown to them. Now that it has begun, we will bring some of them together. Making them aware of the other."

All in his presence acknowledged with a nod.

"We come to uncomplicate what the humans in the realm of time have complicated. It is what they do. We do not blame them; their thoughts are limited. When they chose to cover their terrestrial body, they also put a veil

over their hearts.

"Here in the ethereal realm, you understand there are no divisions by stature, nor religious beliefs or nationalities; we are united. Angels and Spirit guides are as one. All in the ethereal are teachers and enhancers of life.

"This experience that will be created is not the second coming of the Messiah. As so many have been engaged and taught in the realm of time.

"They cannot understand the invisible realm without a physical manifestation. The stars in the galaxies reflect to those in the realm of time to comprehend the realm of spirit.

"We are of the Infinite, not limited to a solar system or galaxy. We exist within pure Spirit that circumnavigates all that is and all that will be.

"Those in the realm of time look to the sky and call it heaven. Yet it is not. They must learn to look within and see heaven does exist. The peace of heaven must be experienced within themselves"

"And what would that purpose be?"

With one voice that vibrated the heavens resoundingly, all shouted:

"JOY"

"Let it be so,"
"Let it be so,"
Their energy raised the vibration within the Universe.
All with one voice declared:

"We are one! It is time for the seekers in the realm of time to see.
It is time for the Lightworkers to shine and share, so there is nothing hidden."
Now it begins....

~*~

Brenna with her coffee in hand headed out of the cabin. Sitting on the porch was her morning ritual. A book on the table by the door caught her attention.

She smiled, lifting it to look closer. "One of mom's books she wrote. Hmm, I don't think I remember reading it. "Now is as good a time as ever. Right, mom?" She called out.

The cover was a simple design, shoes of all kinds nestled together. "Walking in their shoes." *Leave it up to mom to write something like this.* She laughed.

She bumped the door open with her butt holding her coffee and the book in her other hand.

"Ahhh-- Let's see what you created, momma."

<u>"Walking in their shoes."</u>

By Talise Kavanaugh

Introduction

We are unique beings in this realm. All of us are unique in our way, standing out from others to enjoy life. Together we can share the joy. Oh, yes, there is communication that takes place. Yet with some, we aren't of their caliber to comprehend what they are saying. Such as birds, animals of all manner. They share messages, but that is where we have a difficult time understanding them.

You can hear melodies. Are they just singing, or are they sharing a message with others in the trees afar? Either way, it is one of the gifts they have "to communicate." Given to them by the Infinite Spirit.

Our domesticated animals have a way of communicating too. You hear them very clearly by their sounds and their actions. Will you consider this: that others understand us just as well by our sounds and our movements.

<u>Walking in their shoes</u> was a thought that occurred to me since we share so much history.

Many scholars, philosophers, and intellectual beings were never known personally to you, even so to your grandmother or fathers.

I have observed many researching their family lineage. Being aware of this is very encouraging because we learn both genetically and spiritually from our ancestors.

My great-grandmother is always very present to me. Her name-- I don't think that matters to anyone other than me. Always remember yours are with you too.

You must understand the Spirit realm is occupied by many, and though they are many. They enjoy partaking in your life. You only need to call on them. Other beings of times past have something to offer every one of us.

I have been guided to write a short book to make your minds curious about others. This writing is my personal view of them and their life, a sort of journaling for them as they share moments and experiences with me.

How do I do this? I truly have no answers to suffice for you to understand. You can believe the words or just set it aside as a nice fictional book with fairytale-like thoughts within. Either way is truly fine with me. Because I write, when the energy of ideas comes to me for me. For my life and my understanding, that not all is as it seems.

Let us begin…

Each section will be dedicated to one individual at a time. Someone from their family might join in too. Let's see what happens. I think this will be fun.

By Talise Kavanaugh.

Brenna hesitated at what her mother just wrote. She continued to read: "Harriet Tubman, mom? What are you up to?"

<u>Hello Harriet Tubman</u>

"I am pleased you have wanted to visit with me.
It has been a long time since anyone selected me to be with them from your
realm of time."

"Your name came to me, my friend, as I was beginning my book. I am pleased you have agreed to sit with me for a spell.

"As I researched your life, the one recorded on paper and in books, I can see it was one of the most challenging times. Yet you were a powerful black woman to stand out and above many in your time."

I was born into slavery when I was young.
I didn't think I was anything special. I did as my momma told me.
We lived on a large plantation. I would work beside my momma. Back in those days, we grew up very fast. I was, let me see, I think, I think five years old or so. I had to go to a neighboring white owner's home to care for a baby.
I didn't mind this so much, but if the baby cried, they made me cry too.
I missed my momma then so much.
All my brothers and sisters had been treated poorly just as I was. We couldn't live together long; the owners would move us here and there. I tried to keep in contact as I grew older, but we didn't have the new finagled things you all have now."

"I know, this book I am hoping will allow those that have all those new *finagled* things as you say to understand. How life was and maybe appreciate what they have now."

"Girl"… (she laughed)
"They won't know unless they don't have it anymore.
Then they will see."

"I guess you're right, Harriet."

"The world now has no idea what it was like in the 1820s."

"I know, and it indeed wasn't that long ago, if you measure time. Electricity came about in the 1800s, along with Benjamin Franklin just flying a kite with a key on the line.

"This is true," Harriet agreed.

"It was discovered just as many things are guided to or discovered in the realm of time." Harriet continued.

"When I was older, we still used oil lanterns. Most had them. Still, what you are saying is in the 1900's many discoveries were made.

Harriet continued: "Now that I am in the spirit realm, I can look back and see how everything progressed."

"Yes, it did. But with the progression, I think we digressed too. Forgetting what is important." Talise commented.

"Harriet, if you could say one thing to those of us in the realm of time, what would you say?"

"I would say...
Enjoy your family and your freedom.
Many take this for granted."

"Harriet, your story of saving so many from slavery risking your own life is shared worldwide. Our children have learned of your journey. You are most assuredly one of the most beloved people in all cultures. I am truly honored to be with you this day."

"You can call for my presence anytime.
I will be there.".

"I will remember this, in a few years, this is something that will be shared with the world, my friend."

~*~

Hopefully, this will make you the reader inquisitive to understand this lovely caring woman. Her life continued into 1913, touching others. She passed from pneumonia and is remembered by many for saving their lives—May we all not live our lives selfishly, but looking out for each other as she did. Go back and remember to appreciate what you have this day.
Signed:

Talise Kavanaugh: (The Beholder)

~*~

Brenna held her place in the book. She took a moment, sipping her coffee. "What are you up to, mom?" She repeated. You did this such a long time ago. Was this the doorway for you to touch so many over the years?

She knew in her heart it was; she had no idea this book was the gateway to a new chapter in her world too.

The wind from the lake brisked over her hand. She was in deep thought. Knowing she had to continue to read.

Her hand flicked through the pages seeing so many names within it. Mom had to have something in mind when she wrote this. Did she use her intuitive gift to visit these people?

So many questions were surfacing. I guess this is what was meant at The Haven. We had much to learn.

Brenna turned the next page:

What the??

~*~

Hello, Burl Ives

"Hello, Mr. Ives, I must tell you I am so very pleased to be with you."

He smiled his cute smile that I remembered from a child.

"I am pleased to be with you. I see you're engaging many of us to share experiences in your lovely book."

"Yes, I am. I am hoping to engage those that read it to look into the past. Possibly they can take the wisdom of it to their present life.

"Can you share a little of your life with me? I have read the history archives, but I would love to hear it come from you directly."

"Yes, of course. Young lady, are you aware my full name is Burl Icle Ivanhoe Ives? " Now, you know when I began my journey, they had to shorten that!"

"Yes, I see why that would be."

(He laughed.)

My life's journey was mostly entertainment.

Radio, television where ever I felt I would be able to make someone smile. I tried to always go in that direction."

"When were you born?"

"I was born in 1909.

My parents lived in Illinois, and I had quite a large family.

Four sisters and two brothers. We lived on a farm, my father, with all of us, worked the land to provide for the family."

"Times in the early 1900s were very hard as I have read."

"Yes, they were,

and we all worked together to make ends meet.

We were like the 1900 similar to the Walton's that so many that will read this book are familiar with."

I laughed. "Yes, I do remember the Waltons."

He laughed too.

"As I recall, one day, I was in the field and started singing a tune. I did that a lot. My mother loved to hear me sing. This one day, my uncle was nearby, and let's say he was surprised to hear my voice. That's how it all began. He took me to a local gathering, and everyone surrounded me with pats on the back. Commenting on how they never knew I could sing."

"So, that's how it began, right?"

"Yes, it just flowed to one job after another
to become who I was always destined to be."

"What a joy to hear from you, Burl. I have such fond memories of you growing up. I loved listening to your voice. Whether you were telling a childhood story or singing a lovely song to make the little one's smile. You were one of the joy makers of the world.

"What would you say to those in this realm, reading my little book now?"

He thought for a moment, rubbing his mustache. He winked at me, and I laughed.

"I would say, sing…
Share your music no matter where you are.
Your journey is to share your gifts. If it is a song, then do this. It will not
only make you smile but those that listen to you too."

"I agree." (With a deep sigh). I wish and hope others will see that our journey is to find that joy. To enjoy life to the fullest."

"Yes, my dear, I will ask for that too.
When I came to the spirit realm, I smiled, looked back at my life, and
said aloud. That was fun!!"

(Laughing) "I can hear you shouting it out over the mountain tops."

With a quick tip of his head and another wink, he walked away.

"I will see you again. My dear friend, I will see you again!!"

Brenna grabbed her cell phone.

"Maggie?"

"Hon, are you alright?"

"I'm not sure, and I think I am. Did you know about this book mom wrote years ago?"

"Which one?"

"Walking in their shoes." She shouted!

"Of course. That's an old book, written before she even met Nathaniel."

"Have you read it?" Brenna asked.

Maggie laughed. "Are you okay? Do you need me to come to the cabin? I can if you need me."

"No-- I'm confused, maybe." Her voice was a little concerned. "Can I come there?"

"You are always welcome; this is your home, love. Come anytime."

"Okay... I'm going to-- I'm going to finish my coffee and shower. I will be there in an hour or so."

"Alright, I will be waiting."

"I'm bringing this book!" She said as she held it up, being in disbelief of what it contained.

"That's what I figured."

She dialed again.

"Laura? -- As if asking a question. Laura!" She repeated it.

"Yes, it's me."

"I found something here, and you're not going to believe it!"

"What? Are you alright?" The excitement in her voice made Shadow jump.

"I found this book; mom wrote it a long time ago. That's what Maggie said anyway. I guess even before she met dad!"

"I can hear something in your voice; I can't tell if it is excitement or concern!"

"Both!! I guess." She took a deep breath.

"Do you want to talk about it?"

"Have you ever heard of her book titled Walking in their shoes?"

Laura was still for a moment. She had heard of it. Talise shared the story of her life, and it had been briefly mentioned.

"Have you?" Brenna asked.

"I know about it. Is it still in print? I thought it was out of print or something."

"No... no, it's not. I don't think so anyway. I will have to check and see. God, I have this huge headache now. I opened this book, and it just shocked me!"

"Was it bad, I mean, out of your mom's character? Like sex stuff or something." Laura teased.

Brenna laughed out loud, and so did Laura. She needed to find some humor at this moment, and this worked.

Brenna took another deep breath and sipped her coffee, even though it was cold now.

Brenna yelled out. "Chan eil fios agam dè bha màthair a 'smaoineachadh!!"

Laura laughed even louder. "Whoa, girl, I think that verbiage is a wee bit out of my reach. Translate, will ya!"

Brenna laughed, "Oh shit, sorry. I don't know what my mom was thinking!"

"Which of those words was shit? I want to save it for later!"

"None of them! Shit is shit in Gaelic too."

Now they both laughed.

"I'm already on my way there. I just got off the phone, making reservations at the Haven. Joe's coming too."

"Alright."

"God, Brenna, you had me concerned. Go see Maggie. She'll calm your Irish blood."

"Yes, I am going as soon as I hang up here."

The open book was still on her lap. She had to look inside again. Do I dare? I have to-- she opened it up and yelled loud enough for people across the lake to hear her.

"O mo mhàthair dhia!!!" (*translated: oh my god, mom!*)

"Plato... really, Plato??? What the heck were you doing?"

She read a bit more:

<u>Plato</u>

As I walked into the spirit realm, I knew this individual would be one that would take a bit of time to connect with if it was even possible. I would have to be patient.

A shuffling was taking place behind me; I turned to see a man dressed in white apparel. There was a soft, gentle glow around him. I knew I was going back further in time than I had with the others, so this was a new experience for me.

"I am here."

A deep voice announced his presence.

She slammed the book shut. Unsure if anyone else was reading it. She laughed, of course, no one else was reading it!!

Or so she thought.

~~*

"Is she going to be alright?" Nathaniel asked Talise.

Talise hugged him, laughing so hard.

"She's going to be fine. Now is her time for her awakening."

"I remember that book. I don't think it upset me so much."

"I remember," she said.

"I guess you thought it was just a bit of history, aye?"

Well, shit is shit in whatever language you say shit--

They both laughed so hard!

~*~*~*~

Chapter Four

Maggie was waiting for what she knew would be a very excitable red-haired woman to enter her café.

She brought her book out to the table and set a basket of muffins beside it. "There --- I hope these will calm her just a bit." She smiled, understanding Brenna had the same reaction we all did when Talise first wrote this book.

~*~

Maggie knew she was going to be the one to share many things with Brenna. Nathaniel and Talise had kept her protected from the world of her mother. So, she could develop her own creative life. Not feeling they should tell her to do this or do that. They loved her free-spirited ways.

People were entering the restaurant sporadically. She hoped she and Brenna could have a bit of privacy to answer all the questions Brenna would have.

The door swung open with a rush of wind. Maggie laughed, seeing Brenna was behind the noisy entry. Her hair was all messed and tied back with a scarf.

Maggie laughed. *"Thanks, Tally. Your red-haired beacon is lit brightly today."*

She looked around and spotted Maggie. Maggie pulled a chair out for her. With the book in hand, she looked like a little girl that just discovered a hidden treasure.

"Have a seat. Let's talk."

Brenna placed the book roughly on the table in front of her.

"Calm down and take a breath, love. It's fine. Did you think that the gathering you partook in with your parents at the Haven was only to celebrate Samhain last year?

"All is for a purpose, and you are an essential participant."

Brenna was soothed, hearing Maggie.

"You are still adjusting to your mother's transition. It is natural for you to be very emotional. You're not alone. You can come to stay with me if you like until you feel more yourself. I would love that.

"I know you saw that night all the spiritual family that came to the gathering. Yet we are still in the realm of time, and yes, we do need many things that the spirit realm can't provide for our senses, such as touch." -- As she reached across the table and held Brenna's hand.

Brenna's face became flushed; she was trying to hold back the tears.

"Mary, can you bring my niece a cup of coffee, please. Put some of that special flavoring in it too."

"Sure… it's on its way."

The soft music played in the café, soothing all who came in. Maggie hoped it would be calming to Brenna.

The large mug rested in front of her as she put her hands on it to warm them. Her head bowed toward the table.

The silence between them calmed Brenna. Then the café door opened, and another came to their table. It was Allura. All three were bonding that day, a bond that never would be broken.

~*~

Allura brought her book too.

Brenna was surprised. "Did Maggie call you?"

She shook her head, no.

"Then how did you know?"

"That you will understand at a later time, love."

The three women sat, trying to anticipate who would begin.

Brenna lifted the book. "Who's going to start?"

Maggie turned to Allura. "I think this needs to be done in the best way possible. What do you say, Allura?"

"I agree."

"Then let's go to my place."

The three agreed. Maggie let the staff know she was going to her house. As they were getting ready to leave, the front door opened quite briskly.

"Can we join you?" Laura came rushing through the front door... Joseph and Timothy were right behind her. Shadow made his presence known with his wild tail flailing everywhere.

They all had a *sobby* group hug.

~*~

"Follow me," Maggie led them down the stone steps leading to her cottage.

It reminded Brenna of the cottages in Ireland. Quaint with painted shutters. The only thing missing was the grass roof.

When she opened the door, the most beautiful cat greeted them.

"She's beautiful!" Laura said, stroking her long white fur.

Maggie agreed: "She's been my friend forever.

I don't remember how long, quite some time, though.

Her name is Sassy."

Sassy's purring welcomed all to her world.

Joe had Shadow beside him. It was apparent they knew each other. Then Joe felt a soft touch on his hand. It was Brenna reaching for it. He took hold of it to assure her he was right there. And he was going nowhere.

"Let's go in here," Margret guided them to a bright dining area. The sliding glass doors led to a lovely patio. The sun shined brightly into her home, encompassing the perfectly placed table. The room was embellished with plants of all kinds. Laura smiled; all sorts of stones were strategically placed throughout the room.

"Here, Brenna, sit here," as Maggie pulled a chair out for her. She smiled when she noticed Joe holding her hand. "Joseph, you sit right here," (so he was right beside Brenna.)

Allura and Laura couldn't help but notice the hand holding. She was a bit surprised, unaware of the close connection they made when they were last here.

Joe winked at Laura. She nodded with a snicker and raised her brow.

Brenna laughed out loud. "I needed that,"

"Me too!!" Laura laughed.

"What's so funny?" Allura wondered. "Did something happen?"

"Life," Maggie teased, "just life."

"Ohhh, I get it."

The three books rested on the wooden table. Maggie lit a candle. "So, my lovely family, we have something of importance to discuss here. Let's begin.

"Talise, Allura, and I have been friends for years. My connection came through Laura's grandmother Judith. She and I knew each other when I was a young lass. I worked at the publication department at The Women's Life Magazine."

She waited for a moment to see if Laura recognized the name.

"Wait, isn't that where my gram worked?"

"Yes, it is. I was wondering if you knew."

"My friend Tim gave me a letter from my gram that she wrote when she worked there. He found it jammed in the back of a drawer in a desk. That's how he and I met. It was written to me. Then he found me."

"Whoa, there's certainly been a lot here of connecting the dots!" Joe teased.

Everyone laughed. "That's life, and everything is connected. Like the photographs you take. Aren't they a bunch of dots, Joseph?"

He thought for a second, "Oh, you mean the pixels?"

"Yes, I do. The pixels are connected so that you can

see the picture, correct? That's what we are doing here and all try to do within this realm. Connect the dots to see the larger picture."

"I never thought of it like that," Joe commented.

Laura was also grinning, realizing the story was coming together for her too.

"So, how did all of you come to Saol?" He asked.

"Oh, Joseph, patience, patience. We'll get to that."

Allura spoke up. "Right now, we need to discuss this." Holding up the book.

Brenna was calmer now, listening. Knowing these women had her answers.

~~*

Vivian and Talise were, of course,
listening to everything that was taking place.
"Do you think they will tell her everything?"
Talise laughed, "If they do, they'll be here till sunrise."
They both giggled together.

Allura continued. "I knew Talise when she lived on the Island. We grew up together. She was my best friend from the moment we first met. I think that was in first grade.

"I traveled a bit after I graduated, learning from spiritual teachers all over the world. Occasionally my mother would come with me. She was my motivating force then. She was preparing me for what I am doing now, in Shaman's Cove. I had no idea then. It was just great fun.

"On one of my visits home, Talise came over; we sat for hours sharing what had been taking place in our life.

"She noticed I was putting another list together of places I wanted to visit. Tally saw the list and, without hesitation, said. "I'm coming too!"

"When I returned home, my mother had taken over Shaman's Cove. My grandmother was frail and very close to transitioning. We moved to Saol. It was what families did then.

"Talise and I went on our separate ways for a time.

"Wait because I am getting ahead of myself."

"On my last long trip, we finally were able to do this together; we had so many life-changing moments and experiences one could never begin to imagine.

"Remember your first visit to my shop?" (Looking at Joseph and Laura,) "The things I shared with you at the Cove were things I had begun to learn on this trip with Talise. I know your mom taught you privately all that I am sharing here, Brenna.

"From meditation to rocks and herbs, we both had notebooks full of information we had gathered. We always had a pencil and paper.

"That's why Brenna, when you went to Ireland and opened an apothecary shop. Your parents couldn't have been more pleased.

"Our trip; is connected to this." (As she held the book up again.) "We visited the Amazon rain forest."

She waited for that to sink into their minds.

"The tribes and the culture there were profound. We were able to meet a few Shaman and Medicine workers.

"Yes, we came upon some tribes that weren't the ones we would have wanted to connect with. Our guide was as careful as possible, taking us on our expedition.

"Some tribes have not been touched by the world outside. I won't share the name nor the location of them.

This information is not for your research; it's for your understanding of why this book impacted so many people all over the world.

"We were introduced to the hidden magic that is present in this realm. It is beyond what any of you ever could begin to imagine. The beauty, the colors, and landscapes make an artist's palette crave to paint or create such breathtaking colors.

"The animal habitat was unbelievable, seeing it up so close from the smallest microcosms to the majestic elephants."

"We went in twice, and one of the times, we got caught in one of the regularly occurring storms. Luckily we weren't too far from a village."

Everyone was intrigued listening to her story.

"I never knew this, Allura!"

"I know, hon, your parents wanted you to find your own path."

"Was grandma okay with all of this traveling?"

"Sure, she was, your grandfather wasn't concerned either. They both were very aware that Tally was going to be the interpreter of life. Whom the world would call the Beholder, how could she be unless she was out there?

"And *beholden*" …. Maggie added with a chuckle. "She had to BE-HOLD life. Or she couldn't be the Beholder!"

The sun was high in the blue sky you could see through the glass windows. The water in the lake was crystalline blue. A few fishing boats were out enjoying themselves.

It was time for a bit of a break. Everyone could feel

it. Brenna had a smile on her face watching the fishermen out in the lake. She was lost in the experience.

Joe tapped her arm. "Are you okay?"

She squinted her nose with a smile.

He whispered to her, "your mom did that all the time, you know."

It made her smile brighter.

~~*

"See, Vivian, they're doing fine.

I see a wee bit of magic going on with Joseph and Brenna."

"But, of course, we'll have to encourage her to make a sausage pie." Viv laughed, "The way to a man's heart is his stomach."

"I don't think food is what those two have on their minds."

~*~

"If you want to continue, maybe we should have some dinner first," Maggie whispered to Allura.

"Brenna quickly said, "oh, that would be grand. I am starving!"

The books rested on the table where they left them. Their door of understanding was opened.

When they returned to the cottage, Brenna

continued. "When I was a little girl growing up in the cabin. I remember someone coming to me. I thought I was dreaming as I look back on it. Maybe I wasn't.

"So… my mother was taught to do this when she was in the rainforest?"

~*~

Allura continued:

"The town of Manous is where we flew into. It was very alive. We both smiled when we heard it was called The Paris of the Tropics. Our itinerary had already been created, and this was the main access point for visiting the forest."

"Astonishing!" Joe said.

"Yes, it was, and that's where we both came home with lessons. There is so much to experience and see out there in the world.

"Your mother learned about Shamanic life. She never spoke of it too much. You must realize to know of any cultures or ways of life. You must experience them. So, we did. We walked, we listened, we took to us what was right for us and left the rest.

"As you know, there is dark and light in all religions and beliefs. We called to us the light, and that guided us."

She held the book up again. "Talise wrote this as she experienced it. Thus, as she did with all her writings and interpretations, she shared with others."

"Each of the people in the book she actually met?" Brenna asked.

Margaret and Allura again said, "Yes."

"How?"

"It was a gift she was given to be able to look beyond the barrier of this realm."

All were speechless.

"This book opened her door to her path to teaching everyone. To attempt to share what they had forgotten through time. To make the unbelievable believable again.

"Talise loved learning; the more she learned, the more questions she asked. Her awareness of the angels' presence with her since a young girl was one of her strengths. Yet, to convince others of their existence to be able to bring them into reality was not an easy task. In all she did, she never gave up.

"As she matured in confidence, often, she would mingle with local people. Just chit-chatting about this and that. Becoming aware of the gift she had.

"She was interpreting their lives to see how they could look at life differently, just as her mother and grandmother before her did in their own ways."

A joy of understanding surrounded them. Then a bright light shined outside the window. Was it a star? No, it was a glowing orb that turned to hundreds of twinkling lights, like fairies playing with those in the realm of time.

Chapter Five

Laura returned to Boston after a few extra days of relaxation for both her and Joseph.

Timothy rented a car and went back to Boston before her. His business needed his presence.

A peace came over her; she knew what was going to take place. Still, there was no rush. It would be similar to planting a field of seeds. To harvest, to nurture, and take care of those brought to her and Brenna.

Brenna was still at the cabin, adjusting to her new life. Just like Laura was in Boston. The only difference was she had found an unexpected connection to Joseph. He found it with her too.

The spring of the year was beginning. The trees were budding, and the moments from last year were still evident in everyone's minds.

An elderly gent came to Saol.

He was just driving about in his aged car, not having anywhere, in particular, to go. He was enjoying just breathing the fresh air through his car window.

His wife had passed the summer before, and he felt he had to continue.

How to do that? Travel-- and meet people and see what was out there that he and she never seemed to have the time to do.

"Welcome to The Journey," Maggie said as she helped him open the door to her café. (She had been sitting on the bench outside watching the people.)

His hair was gray with age, and his skin pale. His smile lit up the room, thanking her for her kindness.

Many came to Saol as this man, all just wandering the land, Not realizing there would be a little bit of heaven right over the hill.

"Can I pour you some coffee, sir?" She jested with a bit of her Irish accent.

He laughed, hearing her-- "Of course, that would be lovely. Is that blueberry pie I smell baking?"

"Yes, it just came out of the oven. Would ya like a piece?"

"Ohhh, my Sara always made the best blueberry pie."

Maggie knew what he meant, though the words were unsaid. She smiled, knowing full well his Sara was right beside him even though he wasn't aware.

More guests came in, and none were like this gentle little man and the energy that came from him. They were, of course, tourists. You can sense them; they are always in a rush. Never really taking time to enjoy the moment.

Maggie served his pie and coffee. She inquired how long he would be visiting.

"I'm not sure yet. I never know from one moment to the next what direction I'm taking."

"If I can be of help, let me know." She walked away to greet the other visitors.

He watched her from a distance. *I will, he says* softly, *I will.* He turned the magazine resting on his table over. The cover had a photo of someone he seemed to recognize.

He called for Maggie. "Is she here? Does this woman live here?"

"Yes, she did. She was quite a lady and touched many people. Did you know her?"

"I did. I met her a long time ago with my wife. What I would give to spend a little more time with her. My

Sara always made me go wherever Talise was appearing."

"Your Sara must have guided you to come back to us today."

"Do you think so?"

"Yes, I truly do."

"Maybe I should find a room and see why."

"There is a lovely Oak Tree bed and breakfast up the road. I'm sure there is a room there for you. Would you like me to give you the address?"

"I would, I surely would."

"May I ask your name, sir?"

"Joseph. I am Joseph McGrath."

"Well, it is my pleasure Joseph McGrath to meet you."

"McGrath? That sounds familiar. Where have I heard that before?" She thought.

~*~

The day continued as all days do. Since the Beholder documentary presentation, people from all over the world would come just to get a feeling of Saol, but mostly Lake Aisling. That was a huge attraction. It was hard to find a time that the village wasn't busy with humans and vehicles going up and down the hills.

Brenna noticed the increase in people too. Hoping this wouldn't change the unique village her mother loved so dearly.

It is a gathering love, the voice within her shared.
Some are genuine seekers, and others are just visitors coming in and out.
These are the people we spoke to you about.

~*~

Back in Boston: Laura enlightened her boss Tom. On what the latest development was.

"Really?" He sarcastically commented. "Is this anything to do with your last documentary?"

"She hesitated, yes, in a way, sir."

"I don't know, Laura, that was quite extraordinary. Our viewers will be hungry for some of the same stuff."

"Yes, I agree."

"By the way, I never had a chance to ask you. Where did that ending come from with Talise closing it out? I don't remember seeing that in the pre-release viewing."

Laura smiled. "No, sir, it wasn't."

"Well, then how?"

She glanced away and then back.

He seemed to know what she was claiming happened. He smiled. "Really?"

She nodded her head.

"She was the real deal, then?"

Again, she nodded

With a surprised look, he said. "I'll be." He turned

and looked out of the window.

"Well, I'll be." His voice softened now with no sarcasm. "Go ahead, do what you need to, and try to keep me informed. If this is as you say, then I'm totally in agreement."

"It will be another feather in the station's hat, so to speak," Laura said.

~*~

Brenna reached for the empty journal resting on the table by the fireplace. The seasons were well into their change; a new year had begun, and the brisk spring air surrounded her little cabin. Now it was hers, a home to find her serenity and discover her tomorrows.

She smiled, thinking, this is much different than Ireland. Is this to be my new home now? The years she experienced in Ireland did seem to pass by quickly. Her heart felt heavy, realizing back then her communication with her parents was limited. Why didn't I call or write more? She thought.

Her pencil flowed across the blank pages.

Write it down, keep writing it down,
she would hear the voice within say.

Mom, I'm sorry. I'm sorry I didn't write or call more. I know. I guess I felt you were alright with your busy schedule. Yes, your cards made me smile with the photos of all the people you were meeting.

When Dad passed, I felt a piece of me went with him. I think I needed to find that piece of me.

There were many times I almost came home. I wanted to have you hold me. I felt that that would probably keep us both anchored in sadness. I didn't want that.

She rested the pencil on its side, staring at what she wrote. "Is this how you do it, Mom?" She said out loud. "Will this make me feel better? Anchored, that's quite a word, aye? That's how I am feeling anyway. Do you hear me? I know you do."

A voice behind her said: "It's the perfect word."

Brenna turned to see her mother standing in the kitchen. Seeming to be making herself a cup of tea. "Yah, want one, my love?"

"Mom!!?? I knew you were here."

"Hi, baby girl. I love it when you write. You should do it more. It was my way of life--write this write that. Sometimes a lot and sometimes just little thoughts on whatever was nearby." (Talise laughed)

"There were some pretty thought engaging words on those little slips of paper."

Talise continued: "With all my books, it was quite a lovely experience writing them. I would light a candle and say a prayer. Mainly in these latter days. The guides in Spirit that were gifted writers would come to me. I always smiled as my fingers tapped the keyboard putting it in a program on my computer. All my original writings were always on paper with a pencil.

"Then they would be playful and add more to the story. It's a family gift- you know that. Of course, you do." (Her laugh was the same, as it filled the room.)

Brenna seemed to be numb, sitting there watching her mother.

"Awe, come on, relax. This isn't new to you. Do you want me to have Harriet or Berle come say hello?" She giggled.

"No!! ---- Mom, don't do that."

"Alrighty, then, let's have some fun. Let's go out by the water, but first, drink this nice cup of tea. It's a wee bit chilly. It still chills outright to the bone out there. At least for you, it would be but…"

Brenna laughed, "no bones, right, Ma?"

She winked at her daughter, "right."

She walked towards her mom, holding the journal to her heart.

"Where I abide now, the view is much clearer. Easier to explain the whys. It is quite breathtaking."

They sat across from each other, waiting for the other to speak.

"No, your Dad isn't coming today. (She read Brenna's thoughts) He did say to give you his love."

Brenna laughed because she was wondering if he would.

"Touch me," Talise told her daughter.

Brenna moved her hand across the table. Their hands touched seemingly flesh to flesh.

"All can be as you see it or want it to be love. You see me as your mom, and I am.

"There now-- take a breath.

"This is our mother-daughter time. We didn't have that much as you got older. We will make up for the lost times in the years ahead. I promise you that!

"Mother nature has many gifts to give, although someone has to gather them and make humans aware. You saw it with your apothecary in Ireland.

"For myself - my words and my books were my gifts. How about you? How are you, my daughter?"

"I guess I'm alright. I know this takes time to adjust. I am trying to figure out what I am to do now, or even tomorrow."

"I know it all happened so quickly. Spring is here, and soon nature will be bringing forth new life. All the seasons reflect what we can use as a somewhat calendar for our life. Each person has a favorite season, if you ask them.

What would you say is yours?" Talise asked

"The fall, it has always been the fall, life-changing and so colorful and bright."

"Mine too-- I feel the most at peace in the fall. That's why Vivian and I turned our pages of life then. It was time. Time to hand all over to you and Laura."

They walked out to the water's edge, hand in hand.

"So, do you think you will be staying in the village for some time? Have you decided?"

"I was thinking of retracing *your* steps a bit. You

know, like going back to where gram and gramps were. Just observing and sensing all our family had gathered and experienced while they were here."

"Hmm-- that seems like a good idea. I know there are still treasures hidden by them in New England. Do you want to be a treasure hunter? I could help if you want, just like placing my book so you would find it. (She giggled). Everything happens in its time. Always remember that.

Don't forget you have the plans on the parchment given to you at the gathering. You and Laura will accomplish this together."

"Yes, I remember. We have them in a safe place.

"I see you read my book or started it."

"I know it concerned you a bit. At the time when I wrote my books, you never seemed interested in them."

"I had absolutely no idea. I did have a hard time with it. Maybe if I had read it all those years ago… it would have been different. Was dad aware of it?"

"Of course, he was. We had no secrets from each other. His life was busy with the fire department and taking care of local issues. He would smile and shake his head at me from time to time. But in all that, Brenna, your dad understood me. He did right from the beginning."

"I know there are things that probably could have been concealed more than they were. But you were our concern. We needed to keep you safe. When you're dealing with darkness and light, it is a good decision, especially for our children.

"The darkness in spirit form likes to be acknowledged and observed, and feared. That's why your great-great-grandmother Debra tried to share this in her writings. Her attacker told her no one would believe her if she said what he did. So, she shared it with the world. That was her way of releasing it, making some aware that there is darkness in this realm. We don't have to fear them because we are of the light. We have many stories that weren't shared. To share them gives the darkness pleasure. So, we will crush them with the sword of truth, so they retreat."

"I have never heard you speak of this much."

"I chose not to since when you do, you give it life. It latches on to thoughts and fears. That's why the world is so misguided in so many things. The darkness latched on whether in politics or religion and sometimes life in general. Do you see?"

"Yes, I am aware, I do see."

"Our essence is of the light; we have tremendous power to overcome the darkness. Just look at the movies and games the world plays on their computers and phones. When one shows a concern, they say, oh, that's only a game. But is it? Many are caught in the web of deceit and aren't even aware. It is like they are in a trance.

"I will leave you with that thought for now. Just remember what you have experienced and learned. Follow your senses you have acquired. They will be even finer tuned as the years progress. You're orchestrating the plan from the ethereal will awaken many."

"Maggie and Allura are two loving kindred, friends that will assist you in this realm. Yet, if your eyes were opened, you would see you have many, many more that are here to help you. Not only for you but everyone.

"That's what we are taking part in. The love and desire to allow those to see clearly. So, they indeed come to an understanding of what their existence is all about and the purpose.

"You have company coming soon, my sweet daughter. I will see you again very soon. Now give me a hug."

~*~

Joe hadn't returned to Boston yet. He knew Brenna was at the cabin. The urge pulled on him to check on her. He had been renting a house by the water now since October of last year. He did travel back and forth to Boston to be with Laura. His priorities now had changed.

He smiled, remembering Talise's playful way with him when they met. *She asked---*"Are you ready, Joseph?"

He replied, yes, not understanding at the time what she was referring to. But he learned in time; he most definitely learned.

He pulled slowly into the driveway.

Brenna was standing by the water.

He smiled, knowing she was conversing with someone. This site became very familiar with him over the past few months. How strange to realize how much he had changed? He was very aware of those unusual moments.

He sighed deeply. I guess this will be my normal pretty soon. *He heard a chuckle from within.*

Chapter Six

Now the process was to begin.

Everyone knew the spirit realm supported their success in this. This would be a blending of the realms that had never been done before in this way.

~*~

The foursome gathered at The Haven.

Laura came in with Shadow following close by. Her hands were filled with boxes containing what she felt were vital for them to begin.

Brenna had a light tan briefcase and a tube-like package under her arm.

Tim carried ledgers and files.

Joe brought in the least. He had a paper bag --- a small brown bag.

Everyone laughed as they put all their treasures on the huge dining table in the main room.

Laura smiled: "Joe, what's in the bag?"

"A very familiar and common thing for you all," he

said. "Oh, let me show you. He opened it carefully, placing chocolate chip muffins on the platter and snickering as he did it.

Everyone laughed hysterically. "This is perfect, Joe;" Brenna hugged him and quickly grabbed a muffin.

"Yes, it is," Laura laughed, following Brenna's lead.

"Just *keepin* it simple," Joe said. "Just *keepin* it simple."

The large entry door banged open.

"Did someone say they needed coffee? I thought I heard someone say they needed coffee!" Maggie called out as she entered. "Didn't you hear it, Allura?"

"Yes, I did-- Now, where are those muffins? I hope you all didn't scarf them down before we got here."

They all chattered around the table, drinking their coffee and enjoying the muffins.

Brenna mentioned, "We need to make a request now.

Maggie, will you do this for us, please?"

The candles were lit on the mantle, and all knew things were going to take place in this little building.

~*~

"Oh, great Infinite Spirit of life...... We call on the four corners of the realms to be with us as we create this in the way it was envisioned in spirit.

Guide us.

Show us.

Be with us."

~*~

Just as her request was released, a soft wind flowed around them all—a glow of sparkling lights seeming to be like fireflies flickering around the room.

You could hear voices faintly whispering to each other.

"Is this the time?"

Another said, "yes, can you see the parchment on the table?"

Everyone's heart was racing, knowing who and what was coming and what would be taking place.

A male voice radiated through the room.

"Abundant blessings to you all."

A man appeared. He was exquisite; the clothes he wore were of a priestly vesture. Stones of all shapes embellished his garment. His hair was shimmering white with a beard streaming down his face.

"I am Phanuel, known as the archangel of hope. All that are with me are spirit beings' architects of times past that have wanted to assist at this moment."

A group of beings gathered beside him and behind him.

"*Our last visit together, as I am sure you remember, was to awaken you. To allow you to see the things that most have never seen while walking in this realm.*

"*As it was in the beginning: for us to bring this experience to all of the earthly. We required humans. It was not just any humans but those who had the gift born within them to see what we needed.*

"*Your family lineage down through centuries upon centuries has instilled within all of you some of these gifts. More helpers will be provided to you in time. They will assist in reflecting and sharing what home is and bringing peace into men's hearts. It is time now.*"

"*Would you mind if we sat for a while with you?*"

~*~

They all stood silently, numb to what was just asked.

Brenna spoke first: "Please, you honor us with your presence."

At first, it was difficult for the six of them to focus and concentrate on their next step. Brenna rolled the parchment out on the dining room table. Everyone circled to take a look. Laura placed the leather-bound book beside it.

"The way I see it," said Brenna. "We have to think out of the ordinary. I know whenever I came up with an idea. I would always do what my mother taught me.

Look above it to get a more expansive view.

"We see it is lying there on the table with drawings and markings, yet we need to look at it as a whole. To grasp the essence of it. Do you see?"

They all listened intently.

"This village is what we have been told needs to be created by gifted beings. Maybe you don't see yourself as having gifts. But trust me by what we have been allowed to see, and remember the last time we were in this room. If we weren't empowered with some kind of a gift, we wouldn't even be here.

"It's a village, and you can see that from the diagrams it is in sections." The drawing was similar to what you would see on an architectural drawing."

"Look there," Joe said. "That looks like a large building." He was careful not to touch the skin of the drawing.

"Here," Laura handed him a soft-tipped pointer. "Use this."

"Yes, you're right, she agreed. "It must be a place for all to gather at one time. Like an outdoor amphitheater, but covered with a roof."

The elderly guide, sensing the confusion that was about to take place, said:

"When you are seeking assistance, you have the ability to call on those in the ethereal for their expertise in architecture or building. Or if you are a composer, you can call on those in

the spirit realm gifted in music.
"All these spirit beings have the gift of building and creating.
Do you see them?"
They agreed.
"Many structures have been created throughout the
centuries for one purpose or another. Such as the tower of
babel, Noah's ark, the tabernacle and Solomons temple,
Stonehenge, and the Pyramids.
Are you familiar with these?"
They agreed.
"The buildings will not be a great stature as those were. It
is a location that can be facilitated on the ley lines with the
intention of a large gathering to teach and inspire many.
"This is a facility that will be duplicated throughout the
world. From the outside, it will look like any other building
that it is near.
"It is what is within that you see not on that paper that is
precious. View this as Miss Brenna has guided you. View
from above, look at the true essence of this.
"Remember, you have the parchment, and you also have the
book that contains all answers needed. This Miss Laura has
in her possession."
They continued to investigate the blueprint of what
was to be. Each took notes
"Now, look, this is going to be quite an undertaking.
Brenna looked around the room. We will gather those
that can make this happen."

Maggie nodded in agreement.

Laura spoke out. "It will be a production. Production to take place within the building."

"I see it," Tim said.

"Yes, I see it like that." Joe agreed.

The lights in the room flickered.
As orbs of light floating around the room, touching each of
them.
"Well done, the voice echoed. Well done. This will be done
from within. This is the beginning of your understanding.
You are ready.
We will guide and be with you."
The humming sound in the room faded.
~*~

"Wow, Tim said. "I have no words only, wow!!"

They all laughed together, not for the last time, but for many more times to come. To allow the world to see all that seemingly was hidden is there for their asking.

~*~*~*~

Chapter Seven

Tim and Laura had rented the Haven. Joe knew he was to be with Brenna at the cabin. None of them wanted to be alone tonight.

Laura called to all as they were parting. "Keep your notebook and pencils handy. You never know when a thought or message will be given to you; write it down."

"Spoken like a true journalist," Joe teased.

"Laura!" Brenna called out as she turned from walking to her car. "This isn't at all what I expected when I came back from Ireland."

Laura laughed, "I know my friend-- I know."

~*~

Brenna had a hard time when they returned to the cabin. Her heart was racing, and her mind wouldn't settle down.

"Let's go out by the water." Joe took her by the hand and guided her out the front door.

"Alright, maybe that will help. My heart is racing."

She told him of her mother appearing to her the day before. "Joe, it was as if she was there. She was making a cup of tea for herself. Then we sat at the table, and I even touched her!"

Joe listened intently and tried to console her. "Maybe she's trying to show you we can have a connection with those in spirit even if it is to touch. Who said we couldn't? The movies or who? I think it's normal, Brenna. Unless you experience it, there's always a block there in our minds to it being possible."

"Do you think so?"

"Knowing your mother, this was what she was trying to show us all the time. Do you remember seeing her by the shore and talking with someone?"

"Yes—"

"We know that it was your father. Right?"

"Yes—"

"Before you arrived, my god, your mother took Laura and me on some mind-blowing experiences. She even took us back to when she was younger. It was a vision of sorts; we saw it as if we were right there."

"I didn't know that! I told her I was going to go back to where my aunts grew up. To retrace and understand what I'm doing. She said there were treasures there to be discovered."

"Let's do that then, and I'm coming with you, Brenna—You were told you were given the gift of creating. You were going to be making it come to pass. You can't do that without the substance needed. Right?"

"Right."

His words calmed her, knowing what her next move was to be. Plus, knowing Joe was coming with her comforted her. They informed everyone first thing in the morning of their plan.

~*~

The drive took about four hours. She made the time pass by sharing so many memories. Mainly how her parents found Saol, then they decided to move there.

"Your parents seemed to enjoy life together."

"They did... life was always entertaining. My father was more contemplative than my mother. My mother just thought something and did it. Whereas my dad had to hash things around in his mind."

They both laughed.

"I think that was inherited or genetics with all the women in your family. They all were bold and unique!"

"I am sure they'll be keeping us company on this trip. I have absolutely no doubt of that!"

Brenna knew where she needed to begin. The lighthouse--- it's where it all started or seemed to be with her great-great-grandmother, Debra.

~~*

Debra, Leah, Lacey, and Talise were sitting by a lovely tree in the ethereal realm. The wind was a gentle breeze and whispered, not in the form of words to be understood off in the distance.

Talise said: "They're at the lighthouse.
Let's soar near them and see what is happening."

~*~

The light from the lighthouse was filling the sky that overshadowed the rock-filled ledge. If memories could speak, anyone who came to this location would hear story after story echo in every coming wave.

Now it was Brenna and Joe's time. To listen and sense the powers surrounding them, giving them the answers, they would need.

"Is this the same one?"

"Yes, it is."

"Wow, I'm impressed. It looks just as it was described in The Memory barrel. It's like nothing changed at all."

"Oh, I'm sure there is more to the story that wasn't shared in my gram's book." She sighed.

Brenna heard a voice within her:

Sometimes you have to start at the beginning,
to get the full story.

"I'll be right back. I left my journal in the car."

Joe was standing in deep thought, remembering the story, and looking off into the distance at the water. Taking a deep breath, he said. "I am ready." Remembering this is what he had to say when Talise took him on his journey with Laura.

"Yes, you are.
I told you this would-be life-changing dear one."

Brenna found the journal she'd brought with her from the cabin. It had been her mother's. The pages, in the beginning, were blank, so she felt it would work for her.

While walking toward Joe, she felt something drop to the ground. It had been placed in the notebook. It was in an envelope. The writing on the front said;

My dream

"What's this?" It wasn't sealed, so she looked inside.

Joe called to her watching her standing still in the parking lot.

"Are you alright?"

"Yes, yes, I am."

By that time, he was coming closer.

"What's that?" He noticed she was looking at a piece of paper.

"It just… it dropped out of this journal.

Joe smiled. "Now it begins, Bren…"

She held it in her hands and waved it in the air. "It says My Dream on it."

"I know it's for you to read."

Brenna tucked it in the inside pocket of her jacket. "I will," she said. "I will."

With the sun setting, the air was getting much cooler.

"Let's go to the Inn and warm up. We can come back in the morning when our minds are a bit clearer and rested.

~*~

The room was very quaint. All the furniture was a mid-century design. Someone lit the fireplace in the room, so it was toasty warm.

Joe knew the envelope was on her mind. "Do you want to read it now?"

She thought for a moment, "Yes, I think I do."

"Then relax by the fire. I will pour you a glass of wine. I'll leave you alone with it and go take a shower."

"Okay--" She loved how he was so caring about her. Their friendship has grown stronger since last summer. It made her smile.

~*~

The envelope wasn't dated, neither was the letter within.

~~*~~

Hello, Laura and Brenna. I wanted you both to read this. Laura, this is the dream I had when I first met Nathaniel. On our first day of the meeting, I told you I would tell you. In time it comes if you are patient. That's why you're holding it in your hands today.

I am sure I have transitioned, and your both will be finding bits and pieces of our lives. This is just one.

It will show you that our connection to those that are drawn to us isn't just from a physical attraction when you meet face to face in the earthly. It is a connection that began at another time in your life.

Possibly another life you lived. Yes, my loves, you have lived many lives.

I won't get into great depth about this at present. I am sure you have felt a "familiar" feeling to a place or a person.

I won't be taking on another earthly form for some time. I have things to do. In time, if I feel I'm excited to take on a new experience, I will.

Here is my story:

It began at the gathering of women in the town where Nathaniel lived. We were just drawn to each other.

So: this is a page from my journal I copied for you both.

What a great feeling I experienced tonight. Everyone was so kind. I am looking forward to the next get together. At every presentation, I always make new friends. I love it.

A very nice man after the meeting in the town hall came up to me. It was funny because he mentioned he heard about my presentation and bought my books before coming there.

There was something familiar about him; I just couldn't put my finger on why. We did seem to have a connection when he walked me to my car. We talked, and he invited me for coffee in the morning, but I declined.

Later in the world of dreams, I was shown why he was familiar. That was very exciting.

Looking back, it was as if I watched on as an observer. Seeing myself lay on my bed, yet I could see reflections around me, Hints of things like a window seemed to be open, and a mist-filled sky was outside.

There was like a vision of woods with a path that led one deeper into the forest in my room. It seemed to be taking place in almost the edge of a galaxy with stars, more stars than I ever imagined one could see.

I thought-- Wake up, wake up, and see what's surrounding you. The form twisted and turned as if restless. Was she hearing me? Would she see what I was seeing?

I wanted her to wake. Was I a part of her? I bent down beside her.

Come with me, see the beauty that is surrounding us.

Just then, a voice whispered behind me. "You are one," you are the part of her that surrounds her. When a spirit being entered the realm of time, the entire essence of her isn't confined. There is a free spirit part of her that stays and isn't restricted.

I had never heard such words before. It seems there are two of you yet; you are one.

You take her to the worlds of dreams. You see things clearer than what she can in the flesh. Those that surround you are spirit beings, total energy. They walk beside you and show you your way."

I said, "I should wake her."

"She is awake," the voice said. "Because you are awake. She will come with you to your dream world as you walk with her in the world of time."

"What should I do?"

"Begin your dream, walk into it, and see what you've to see."

I pulled my robe tighter and walked toward the path. Lights were twinkling all around me.

There was a magical stillness. As I stopped, I couldn't see the woman in the bed. I mean, I couldn't see ME in the bed.

A male voice called, "I'm over here." I followed where the voice called to me. I could smell a fire was burning like in a campfire.

"Come on, you need to come back." The voice called out.

I continued to walk.

Through the trees, I could see a man was sitting beside a campfire. It was apparent there was a place for me to sit.

He heard me coming from behind. I stood there, trying to understand what was taking place. Then he turned towards me.

"I've been waiting, my love. We have so much to do."

"Do we?"

"Yes, we have to......"

As I looked deeper into his eyes, it was him. It was Nathaniel; he came to me.

"I woke before he said what we had to do.
Oh my gosh, when would we meet again? Was he having the same dream?"
Morning came quickly as the alarm rang by my bed. His business card was sitting on my bed stand.
Was this fate?
Had we known each other before?
Yes, I think so. I heard him say we had so much to do! He called me LOVE.

I reached for the phone. I'll call him. He said to call him.
So, I did.

His voice was sleepy as he answered. "Hello?"
"Hi, Nathaniel," her voice was guarded and hesitating. "Is this too early?"
"Ahh... no, no." He was more awake now, knowing it was Talise.
"I just wanted to say. I will take you up on that coffee and muffin. If you still have the time or want to.
Okay-- I'll see you at 8:30.

Perfect.
As we drank our coffee, he confided he had a restless night.
Then what he said, I almost fell off my chair.

"I can't explain all or why, but I do remember building a campfire.
I smiled. I understood it was amazing though he had no idea.
In time he would. In time he would.

Update:

He is such a patient man. I love him to the depths of my soul. My way of life entertained him. He would always say. While you're just out there soaring. I will never be far, my love.

I came back to be with him after I went with Allura, my friend, to South America. What was funny was when I came home. I found him by his home in the woods. Tent and all chairs beside a campfire, one for him and one for me. We married two years later, and we bought a lovely lighthouse.

Brenna put the letter to her heart. Lying back in the chair, she understood. A match made in heaven, mom, right? Now I know why you named me Brenna. It means beacon on a hill. I understand, Mom. I understand.

The voice within said:

You were our light that appeared to us in the lighthouse.

~*~*~*~

Chapter Eight

While the world was becoming very busy for Brenna in Maine. Laura was also feeling the quickening while at Lake Aisling. Both were very aware of what was taking place. The energy flow was inspiriting.

Laura's cell phone rang:

"Are you up and around, or do I have to come up there and carry you out of bed?"

Laura laughed, Tim has always been pretty predictable, and she knew that would possibly happen if she didn't kick out of the covers and get moving.

"I'm coming silly. I'm coming."

"Great, I called Maggie, and she said in about twenty minutes, a new batch of muffins were coming out of the oven."

~*~

"Well, there ya be!" Maggie shouted across the dining room, making her grand entrance from the kitchen. The door swung open and almost clobbered her delicious tray she was holding in her hands. She laughed so hard.

"Aye, ya missed me again." She chuckled as if talking to the door. But if you knew Maggie, her life was filled with fairies and all kinds of playful beings. Some you could see with your eyes and some not. You would always chuckle, watching her mannerisms.

"Hey Maggie," Laura and Tim called back, laughing at her entrance.

"Git over here and give me a hug. Just let me set this tray down first."

She pulled up a chair and straightened her apron. She was brushing some flour off the front of it. There was a little spot on her nose too. Laura tapped it off.

"Well, thank you, love. You both look refreshed well, maybe one of you looks refreshed. Are you alright? Sleeping? Or is your mind just reelin?"

Laura rolled her eyes, "you always seem to know even if the words aren't shared, Mags. I love that."

"Oh, words can be overrated," she shuffled in her chair.

After breakfast, they walked out to the patio that overlooked the lake.

The fishermen were scattered around the lake, trying to get their catch of the day. Some did, and some didn't. Grandiose fish stories always accompanied the seekers as they came to shore. They were always clamoring on the big one that got away.

Homes were minimal along the shoreline on either side.
Lake Aisling was for everyone.
In town, there were novelty shops and local markets filled by the farmers that surrounded it. Vegetables galore, so many varieties you would think it was a village of international origins. Maybe so…

On the balcony, an elderly gent was relaxing with his feet up on the ledge. You could see he was enjoying the view. He turned to look, as he felt Laura watching him. He tapped his hat to say hello. She blushed, being caught, and smiled back at him.

"Do you know him?" Tim asked.

"No, not yet. But my mother would always say the world is filled with friends, we haven't met yet."

Laura touched his hand. She could see he was in another place, not here with her.

"I'm alright, not to worry. The word production keeps flying around in my thoughts. A production?"

Behind them came an elderly voice. Allow me to introduce myself properly if I may be so bold."

"I am Joseph McGrath," as he extended his hand.

Laura reached out first. "It's nice to meet you, sir, and I apologize for staring; I'm Laura Lang."

"Ah, the reporter. I've heard of you."

"Yes, yes, that's me."

"My wife brought me here quite a while ago. It certainly can captivate your creative imagination.

"Oh, did she?" Tim asked. "We would love to meet her."

"She passed two years ago, son. Be sure if you see her, you make sure to let me know, okay?"

All three laughed.

"I'm staying at the Oak Tree Inn up the road. I thought I saw you there yesterday."

Tim smiled. "Yes, you caught me wandering around. I stayed there last year for about a month. I loved it."

"I'm enjoying myself there too."

"So, Mr. McGrath, what brings you to Saol?"

He laughed," I have no idea, but I'm sure I will find out very soon."

"Yes, you will. Would you like to join us for a few moments?"

"If it isn't a bother, I would love to. I couldn't help overhearing you just a moment ago." He pulled a chair out to sit.

"What was that?" Laura asked.

"Production-- I heard the word production."

Tim and Laura looked at each other. With a questioning look on their face.

"Yes, I did say that." Laura agreed.

"I'm always tuned in to words as you are Laura, being a reporter. I didn't hear what you do, Tim?"

"I have been for years in advertising. "

"Wonderful." Joseph playfully chuckled. "The two go together very well."

"You have no idea!" Laura laughed.

~*~

The three agreed to have dinner together very soon. Little did they understand Mr. McGrath was going to be an essential piece of their puzzle. They will all see, very soon!

Tim and Laura decided to take a walk.

"Hey, she smacked Tim. Let's go to Shaman's cove. You've never been in there, have you?"

"No--"

"This shop is something you need to experience."

"It's one of many things I think I need," Tim laughed as he spun her around and dipped her back to kiss her.

"Hey, we're out in public!"

"Yeah-- sooo? Alert the media, will ya?"

She laughed as he gave her one last kiss before letting her go.

They opened the door, and the bell overhead tinkled. The smell of incense filled the shop.

"Hello," a soft, familiar voice came from the back room.

It was Allura. "Welcome, welcome to my world Mr. Timothy O'Farrell. Your first time here, aye? I promise I will be sure to entertain you, so you never forget your first. Firsts are very, very important, you know!!"

She walked them back to the library. Then pulled out the book by Talise: Walking in their shoes. The cover had shoes of all kinds on it. Some antique looking and some were made of rope and string.

"Here ya go, lad, some light reading for ya."

He examined the book. "This is the book you all were talking about the other day."

Laura laughed. "Yeah, light reading, my eye."

Laura took Tim by the hand. "Come on, let's look around. You might find something to want," she said with a snicker.

Allura laughed too, remembering that's what Talise said all the time when she was going shopping.

She rested in her wooden rocking chair, watching the two investigate the cove. It was fun to see Laura pointing out what she had discovered on her first moment here with Joe last year. When they both settled, she moved to the table in the middle of the room of stones.

"I know life is quite busy for you both at the moment. Try to remember you do need to relax and enjoy life. There is no rush to make your assignment. If you stress on it, it will hold you back. You will be given all you need, whether locations, people to assist. All of it. I needed to reassure you of this."

Allura handed him a black stone. "I think you will find this quite beneficial. It is hematite. Have you heard of the energy of stones, Timothy?"

"I noticed Laura has stones around her apartment. I never asked why, though."

Laura pulled her stone from under her top to show she was always wearing one. "This is rose quartz; it's a calming, healing stone."

"Really, does it work?"

"It does for me with other ones I use too."

"This stone," Allura shared, "is one I feel will be beneficial to you, Tim. It is a calming stone too. When you hold it, the stress within you seems to be disengaged.

Try it. Experience it and see. Then let me know what you think when we see each other again.

"There are many elements in this earth plane that are beneficial. If someone doesn't teach you, how would you know.?"

He tucked the stone in his pocket. "I look forward to learning many things from you, Allura."

~*~

Now it was Brenna and Joseph's time to see what was to be revealed on their journey in Maine.

They enjoyed their morning breakfast at the restaurant next to the lighthouse. Their energy was high. Was it from the ocean? Possibly.

Brenna was entranced as she focused on the water with the waves cresting on the rocks below.

"Ya know, she said-- I know my great-great-grandmother sat on those rocks. It was in her journal. This location changed her life, some for good and some for the challenges. Still, she always came back here for her answers. I think I need to re-read her book. "

"Which one?" Josephs said.

"The Memory Barrel, she began it as a journal; her guides convinced her to change the story to make it of true love, the best ever to exist."

"The best to ever exist? Maybe I should read it too take some pointers." He laughed.

More tourists were coming into the small restaurant. It was time to go to their next destination.

"Let's stop at the Inn for a quick moment. I need to get a few things. It is quite a drive to come back here."

"That sounds like a good plan."

The light outside glowed through the sitting room window. Rays of light seeming to be pointing at something for her to view. She smiled, following its direction. It was to a shadowbox hung on the wall. The contents inside seemed to be aged. There it was, The Memory Barrel. Her laughter brought Joseph to see what was so funny.

"Look, Joe."

He shook his head; nothing seemed to surprise him these days.

The innkeeper came out of his back office, hearing her laughter.

"Is everything alright?"

"Oh, yes, Brenna said. I'm admiring the book. I know or was familiar with the author."

"You don't look old enough, sweet girl, to have personally known her."

"She was my great- great- grandmother."

"How interesting! Many visitors have read that little book while visiting the Inn. As you see, it was getting pretty worn over the years. We thought it would be a good idea to protect it. Once someone reads it, they would say they felt the magic of the story. They always came back for years to see if they could experience what she did."

"So, was this the Inn she stayed at all those years ago?"

"Yes, pretty much, we've changed a few things here and there. Many owners have taken it over since then, but this book always stayed."

"The story has been shared over and over. Your great grandmother Leah published the book. Her mother, Debra, had died before it was completed."

"Yes, that's correct."

"May I ask you a question since your family?"

"Of course."

"Where did everyone finally settle to live? They always seemed to love New England. Did everyone settle here in the area?"

"Was the writing a gift that was passed down, or did it end with this book?"

"It was the book that opened so many opportunities for my family. Especially when it became a movie. Everyone did stay in Maine or the New England area.

My mother had a film made of her and her life just last year it was released."

"Your family has been very visible to the world in one manner or another. That is very interesting. What was your mother's name if I may ask?"

"Talise Kavanaugh, she came here when she was a

little girl and when she was older."

"Talise? Did you say Talise? I remember her visiting last year. Yes, yes, she came with a friend. I remember her because it was such an unusual name. Let me think of her friend's name." He called out to his wife. "Honey, do you remember Talise last year?"

"Yes, I do. Why?"

"What was her friend's name?"

She thought for a moment.

"It was Vivian. Yes, she called her Viv. I have it here in the guest log."

She opened the log and went to the previous year. I remember it was in the fall because we were getting ready to close for the season.

"Here it is." She tapped it with her hand. "October--October 5th. We were closing the next weekend. They both seemed to know that."

"I wonder, what were they doing here?"

The innkeeper looked at his wife, wondering if she knew since she did kindle a friendship with them.

"I'm not sure if it was completed or not. I overheard them mention they were signing some papers for a property located on the coastline. They were laughing a lot about it. I did overhear Talise say, now this will be a surprise."

"Really?" Brenna said.

"Yes, yes, I am sure of it."

"How would I find out where it is?"

"Go to the clerk's office in town. I am sure they can help.

Chapter Nine

Joe drove down the narrow road. He wasn't sure what she wanted to do first. Most assuredly, he did know he needed to find the nearest clerk's office.

They pulled into the little village nearby. It had so many similarities to Saol. It was as if the same stores and the appearance of the town existed just in different locations.

He parked in front of the Lincoln county office building. "I'm sure someone can help us here.

"Are you ready?"

Brenna wasn't even paying attention to where he was driving. She looked out the window and saw the signs for the county offices.

"Yes, I am."

"Let's find out if there is anything here you are to be aware of. Your mom told you there were treasures to discover."

Hand in hand, they walked up the sidewalk. You could smell freshly baked goods hovering in the air. They both smiled. It reminded them of Maggie and her baked goods.

"Hey, maybe her sister lives over there. Now that wouldn't surprise me at all." Joe teased.

Brenna laughed, "maybe, we'll check it out after this."

The door was heavy to push open. The building smelled old and musty.

The large plaque on the wall directing where the offices were located. It read:

(Town clerk)

Find me over yonder,

If I'm gone, look for me on the back porch enjoying a lemonade. I'm never far,
that is until sundown.

They laughed, reading it.

"Come on, let's see!"

"Where do you think over yonder is?"

"Not too far, I'm sure."

Soft music guided them to an open door up the hallway.

The door squeaked as Joe pushed it open. A little man sat at the desk, facing away from the door.

He didn't hear them come in.

"Ahh hum, excuse me, sir," Joseph said.

Still, he didn't hear him. He raised his voice a bit.

"Excuse me, sir, can we bother you for a moment?"

He turned in his antique squeaky chair. "No, bother son. No, bother at all. What can I do for you? Do you need a marriage license? It's a good day to get married?"

They looked at each other and laughed.

"Maybe another time we'll be back, sir. For now, we need to check some recent property purchases."

"Oh, too bad-- It is a good day to get married, don't you think?" Smiling at Brenna.

"Lad, she is beautiful. Don't be waiting too long, lots of fish in the ocean, ya know."

"Yes, sir, I will remember..."

They explained their reason for being there.

"Hmm, let's see. October ya say?"

"Yes, sir."

"Two women, ya say?"

"Yes, sir."

He pulled out a card catalog. "We don't use those finangled new *putters*. It is good to do things the normal way. Like this," he pulled out a shoebox filled with cards.

They were amazed. The box was marked: **October**.

"October is a good month. Harvest moon lots of celebrations happenin that month."

Brenna had a hard time containing her laughter.

"Awe, sweet girl, we will find it, not to worry."

He knew just what he was looking for. His old wrinkled hands flipped through the cards like he was a wizard.

"Ahhh, there ya be."

He looked at the card closer: "Talise Kavanaugh?"

Neither of them noticed
that introductions weren't shared.
How did he know their names?
(I am sure you are understanding how.)

"Yes, that would be her."

"Ahh, do I sense a wee bit of an Irish accent, love?"

"Yes, sir, I lived in Kilkenny. I lived there for ten years."

"I know this place," the old gent shared. Kilkenny loves to party."

"It certainly does." Brenna was surprised by his familiarity with it.

"I was there after the war. The art festivals and music are constantly pumping the city with new life, toe-tapping energy. It's a lovely place to make you just feel good."

Brenna smiled, thinking back to her home that she left. Now it seems her life had chosen a new direction for her.

"If it was your home, will you be going back soon?"

"I'm not sure; you see, my mom is Talise, and she passed only a few months ago. I came home to be with her and take care of her.

"Now I found she had purchased something here shortly before she died. I appreciate your help with this."

"Of course, I understand. I am sorry for your loss, lass. I am sure she had you in mind when she purchased this land."

"Land? She bought some land?"

~~*

"She's doing very well. What do you think, love?"
Talise said to Nathaniel.
"Our little girl always sees things through.
"She's going to be pleased when she sees it.
Is the Sage going to visit her?"
Smiling, Tally nodded, "Knowing him, he'll make it not so obvious. Her awakening began last year, so she is more focused. Right now, she's like a baby bird trying to find her way. It will come."

"Yes, this purchase is quite a large area: it sets between Bristol, Pemaquid, and Round Pond."

He pulled a map out to show them. "It is right on the coastline.

"You see? There's a small little pond included in the purchase.

"Take a ride, and you will see the view is beautiful. There aren't many homes or businesses out there. I was curious but never asked why she was looking for land so far away from everything."

"Thank you so much for your help Mr.--?"

"My name is Peter Brindle, ma'am. It is a pleasure to meet you."

"Brindle-- that name sounds so familiar."

"We all stay pretty close in location in this neck of Maine."

"Were you related to Jim and Helen Brindle? They were the innkeepers for the Inn on Pemaquid years and years ago."

His eyes lit up. "I am; he was my great grandfather. I worked as a young lad there for my father when he was taking care of my great granddad."

"I'm sure we will see each other from time to time, Mr. Brindle. If I don't find you in the office, I will know where to find you."

He laughed. "I am sure you shall."

~*~

"Where to Miss Brenna Kavanaugh?" Joe teased.

"Oh, Joseph, Bristol, of course. It isn't far from here. The road is called -- hmm, there doesn't seem to be a road on the map. Only trees everywhere. Let's go closer, then maybe someone can give us some directions. (*Then she remembered Joe saying to the clerk; we will be back later. What did that mean, she thought?*)

As they were driving, a loud sound came from the engine of the car.

"What the heck," Joe said.

It got louder and louder.

"What is it, Joe?"

"I think we've blown a gasket or something."

The smoke billowed out from under the hood.

"Oh no, we are out in the middle of nowhere."

Joe pulled his phone out; there was no reception.

They both circled the car, not sure what their next move would be. Not one car had passed them as they drove here. It was definitely a concerning situation.

"Joe?" Brenna said with tears in her eyes.

He knew she was afraid. "I know, let's just take a moment and sit here on the grass and relax. It will all work out!

He pulled a blanket out and laid it on the ground. Brenna was pacing back and forth. She had a very excitable personality; right now, he had to keep her calm.

"Oh shit, what if we're here until dark? No one even knows we're here!! She yelled. "No one!!" She yelled louder "Mom...cad e an ifreann a bhi tu ag smaoineamn?"

Joe had no idea what she said and couldn't hold back the laugh, hearing her speak in Gaelic.

"It's not funny, Joe!"

"Bren, I have never heard you speak in Gaelic. What did you say?"

"Oh, never mind, my mother, knows what I said!"

~*~

Back in the village of Saol:

Laura was walking along the water at Lake Aisling and suddenly stopped. She heard Brenna crying. She listened a little closer, then it stopped. *My mind is playing tricks on me.* Walking to the table, she started writing on her tablet.

Her pencil moved along the paper. She stopped-- "What the heck?"

She needs you to come to her.

Reading the words, she almost fell off the bench. Grabbing her backpack, she ran into the Haven.

"Tim. Tim, where are you?"

He came running into the grand room.

"What's the matter, are you alright?"

"Yes."

"Good, shit, you scared the crap out of me."

"It's Brenna, and she's in trouble."

"Where?"

"I don't know, but look at this," she showed him the paper.

"Did you write this?"

"No-- well, yes, kind of --the pencil moved my hand across the paper."

She looked back on her text messages she had received from Brenna. Her eyes were racing through them:

"Joes with her, they went on a trip. Now I remember they told us they were going back to discover things about her family. They're in Maine." She yelled, "they're in Maine!"

"Oh crap, but where? What the hell, Brenna, you need to be more careful! I can't fly over you like your mother did to make sure you're alright!"

Yes, you can, the voice within shared.

How? She shouted, tell me how.

Relax

Call to your angels.

Ask them if she is alright.

She asked.

The voice said: Yes.

Remember, you have your sister's connection to her. If she settles down, she will remember.

Send her a message.

Laura closed her eyes:

Brenna, calm down, just calm down!

"Joe?" Brenna said. "Did you say something to me?"

"No."

"I heard a voice. Calm down, it said. Just calm down."

"Then calm down, Bren, it's going to be alright."

Laura could feel her calming. "Now, what do I do?"

Tell her help is coming

She did.

Brenna, my sister, help is coming.

Brenna's eyes opened so wide.

She scared Joe. "Are you ok?"

"Yes. It's like Laura is sending me messages. Telepathically."

"What did she say?"

She said: "Help is coming."

Both ladies took a deep breath. They had never communicated this way before

This is how we do it in the ethereal realm.

~*~

The sun was going down, and though they knew help was on the way. The anxiousness of being in the middle of nowhere was settling in.

Out from the trees, they heard shuffling.

"Oh my gosh, Joe, what do you think it is?"

He stood in front of her to protect her.

"I don't know; it's getting closer," he grabbed the tire iron from off the blanket.

Brenna stood behind Joe with the car door partially open, in case they had to dodge inside.

Suddenly a man's voice shouted from deep within the trees. "Dang it, dog! I'm goin to throw you in the crick if you don't get back here!!"

A beautiful German shepherd came running out of the woods. A little rabbit was just a few leaps ahead of it. Both weren't paying attention to anything but each other. The dog was covered with burdock, obviously from his determined chase to catch the rabbit. The rabbit saw them standing by the car and dodged the other way.

The dog stopped the chase and was staring at the

strangers. He had something else to entertain him now.

Joe had a way with animals, "hey boy."

He poured some water in his hand to show the dog he had water. Without hesitation, he came closer. He put his hand under the dog's chin so he could catch the water for him.

"Ahhh, I see ya made a friend there, dog!" The dog ran to the elderly gent who came out from the trees. "You foolish hound. I am getting too old to be chasing you down. You know there are lots of wild animals out here." (He winked at Joe, knowing Brenna was thinking that already.)

"Really?" Brenna's voice squealed.

The gent's clothes were worn, and his aged hat tipped to one side of his gray hair. His beard was a bit scruffy. You could see he was at home here in the woods.

Joe extended his hand; "I'm Joe McGrath, sir, and this is…"

The elderly gent jumped in and said, "your wife, I presume?"

Joe smiled, "No, sir, we're good friends."

"Ahh, good friend's aye? It looks like you were ready to take on a bear if need be by the size of that tire iron. Maybe it's a bit more than friends?" He chuckled.

Joe smirked at Brenna. Of course, she had a quirky look on her face. This was the second time in a few hours someone mentioned *marriage*.

The Sage named Henry has appeared.

"My name is Henry," he said, tipping his hat at his introduction. He bent down and patted his dog. "And this rambunctious friend of mine is, Hank."

Brenna finally spoke: "I am so thankful to see you, sir, and your dog. We broke down as you can see-- she pointed to the car."

"Yes, ma'am, not many come out this way. Were you lost?"

"No, we were heading towards Bristol. I should have known we took a wrong turn. There were no road markings on the map we were using."

"Young lady, sometimes the roads we take don't need to be drawn on a map. At times they just appear out of nowhere, and you follow them to see where you're being led to. The roads less traveled are the ones you find fascinating things on!"

Brenna thought about what he said, seeming to understand.

"Hank, it looks like we're going to have guests for the night."

"Oh no, sir, we have to get…"

"Now, now, where would you be needin to go this late at night? He knew she was concerned, being a stranger and all. So, he reached in his back pocket, pulling out a radio. The reception buzzed as he clicked it on.

"Hey, is anyone out there? (out)" he said.

Within a few seconds, a voice said: "Henry, what are you up to? You never call us. (out)"

"Oh, you know me, Gladys, I'm a man of few words. (out)"

"Now, if we can get your actions to be like your words, old man. (out)" She laughed.

"Oh, you're just sayin that because your old horny dog wants to have a piece of my Hank. (out)"

Joe and Brenna laughed, hearing them chatter among themselves.

"What do I owe this pleasure. (out)"

"Now listen, Gladys, there's a burgundy Toyota out here on old route 42. Can you let John know so he can arrange for a tow truck to come to help this sweet couple? (out)"

"Sure, I can; he's out fishing right now. It won't be until the morning. (out)"

"I knew that. They'll be my guests for the night. We will be back at the car by 9. That should be enough time for him to finish with his coffee and apple pie and help me rescue Joe and his friend. (out)" (he said sarcastically)

"Where are you to registered at?"

Joe said, "The Inn by the lighthouse."

"Gladys, can you do me one more favor? (out)"

"Only if I can ask favors of you, old man! (out)"

He covered the speaker, "this woman has been after me since her husband passed twenty years ago. She's determined to snatch me up. I'm quite a catch ya know!"

They both laughed.

"Gladys, give the Lighthouse Inn a call and tell them that Mr. McGrath and Miss???"
(Brenna whispered: "Kavanaugh.")

"Miss Kavanaugh are fine, and they'll be returning tomorrow in the afternoon? She wants them to call her family and let them know they're fine. (out)"

"Sure thing. Now don't be feeding them any critters out there, old man. We know you can't cook. (out)"

He turned his radio off and extended his hand towards the trees. "My home is yours tonight."

~*~*~*~

Chapter Ten

There was no way Brenna and Joe knew this was all in the planning. Everything in this earthly realm is synchronized.

Henry's cabin was hidden deep in the woods. The path leading to it wasn't too difficult. The walk was very peaceful. You could hear there was a stream flowing near the cabin.

Joe held Brenna's hand to assure her he was right there, and everything would be fine.

Brenna was positive her mother and others were behind this entire experience. She finally felt safe and was curious to see what was next—nudging Joe as they walked side by side. "You're pretty quiet. What are you thinking?"

"Nothing is just an oops in your girls' worlds. I saw that when Laura and I first came to interview your mother. My god, there were times we were talking, then within seconds, she had us in another place and time. It was always for a reason.

Henry seems pretty personable and all. But trust me, he isn't an innocent bystander. He's got something up his sleeves."

Henry smiled, listening to their chatter.

"Have fun with them, Henry."

"Oh, *I will*," he snickered and stroked his beard.

Henry opened the front door and extended his hand. "My castle," he said.

Oil lamps lit on the mantle gave enough light to see the inside. The cabin didn't have separate bedrooms. It was all one open area.

Hank went right to his blanket that rested in front of the old Franklin wood stove. He was exhausted. It didn't take him long to start snoring and jumping in his sleep. He was probably chasing his rabbit friend again.

"Make yourselves comfortable. I'll throw something together for dinner. I'm sure you're starved."

Brenna looked around. The chairs were old and worn. She remembered chairs and furniture like this when she was a little girl visiting her grandmother.

Henry stomped his foot hard on the floor, "Got ya, ya, little bugger!!" He shouted.

Hank didn't even budge. He was use to Henry stomping around.

But Brenna almost jumped out of her skin.

"I see you're looking over my castle. It's not much, but it's home." He smiled, touching the water pump on the kitchen counter.

"Would you like to freshen up? It does work." He pulled the handle up and down; the water flowed into the bucket under it.

"I know it's been a long day for you. There are clean towels over in the cupboard. The soap is there, too, in a glass mason jar. You know-- the critters like to make themselves at home in cloth. I'll never understand why they like to gnaw at the soap, though." He chuckled.

"Mr. Henry, do you have a bathroom I could use?"

"Sure, do, little lady. I know women like their privacy." He walked across the room towards another door.

Brenna sighed a breath of relief, seeing there was another room with a door on it.

She quickly followed him having to go to the bathroom, really bad.

He opened the door.

"What's this, sir?" She said with concern. Do you

want me to go in the trees?"

"Heck, no! What do you think we are here--animals?"

He tugged her hand outside and pointed to a newly painted outhouse.

Her heart sank. Joe was doing everything to contain the laughter.

"Not to worry, little lady, Hank keeps the critters away from this. You have nothin to concern yourself with."

She hesitantly walked towards it. The door squeaked as she peeked into the cracked opening.

The sign on the door said:

What happens in the outhouse-
Stays in the outhouse!

(Now you know Joe was holding back the laughter, especially when he heard the squeals come from inside.)

Henry walked past Joe and winked.

~*~

Whatever that old man was cooking smelled heavenly. The aroma was seeping out the windows and cracks to tantalize any passerby. He chuckled, knowing this was concerning to them both. He continued tossing the vegetables in the pan as they cooked on his propane stove.

Brenna came to the table, holding on to Joe's arm like a child. This experience was definitely bringing them closer in trust, plus seeing he would always take care of her. He whispered something in her ear, and a huge smile appeared.

Joe was the first to take a bite. He raised his eyebrows and winked at her, showing her, it was acceptable to eat.

After the dishes were cleaned, by hand in the bucket by all, Joe thanked Henry for his hospitality.

"Yes, thank you, Henry."

Henry pointed to the corner of the large room. "There are blankets and pillows in that wooden chest over there."

"Brenna sighed, "Let me guess, that's how to keep the critters out of them?"

Joe and Henry laughed.

The sleeping arrangements were snug. Brenna wasn't going to let Joseph out of her sight. He knew this.

"Come on, babe," he said, patting the cot. I'll be right next to you."

She snuggled up to the wall as he held her close, whispering to her. "The morning will come soon. Close your eyes and know I'm right here."

~*~

Henry appeared to her in her dream. However, he didn't appear as she saw him before. Tonight, he was her teacher and guide.
She listened to his words.

"*As with all dreams, you will only remember a piece of this moment. In time it will all come back to you for you to understand.*

"*Are you aware of the blending? The blending of the realms?*" *He asked her.*

She replied: "I have never heard it explained this way, but I do think so."

"*This is good.*"

Brenna was unsure what was going to take place.

"*You're dreaming,*" *he told her.* "*Dreams can be enlightening; you have nothing to fear. See your safe,*" *as he pointed to a woman sleeping in the bed.*

Joe was sleeping soundly beside her.

"Can he hear us?"

"*No, he has his journey the same as you. You will be walking side by side in many moments.*"

In another lifetime, Joseph was a good friend to you."

"Really?"

"Yes, we all have had many life experiences; each one carries a bit of a glimmer to another. You're not just a soul having one body experience. You have, and all have had a variety of experiences in many years prior, and yes, many more to come."

The thunder cracked; "a storm is coming, follow me."

His attire was elegant. His robe was long and white with gold trim. His hair streamed long and smoothed down his back. The wind blew through it as he paced his steps.

They walked along; she was focused on not losing him in the woods. Yet, now she sensed someone else was beside her. She glanced to her side, not losing her pace. There was a lovely woman clothed in white with a fur like cape resting on her shoulders. A glow surrounded her as if the light of energy was magnetized to her very being. Beside her were two beautiful dogs.

She thought they appeared to be white wolves.

The beautiful woman smiled towards Brenna, letting her know she was aware of her presence.

A sound came from her other side to make her

aware of someone else was there---The hood of his tunic almost covered his face so that she couldn't get a good glimpse of him. He was a dark complexion male, with the most beautiful array of fine jewelry around his neck.

Something moved on his shoulder. Being hesitant to step out to see what it was.

He raised his left arm as if encouraging his companion to walk forward. It was a beautiful hawk, with a small golden amulet on its head.

It nodded to Brenna.

She acknowledged with a nod back.

"Here we are. Follow me," the sage guided.

The thunder cracked again, strong enough to make the ground vibrate this time. No sooner were they inside, and the heavy rain showered the land.

The cave glowed with orbs of light floating around. Some almost seemed to be playing with the other.

"Have a rest here, my dear," as he pointed to a large boulder.

Her new companions stood at her side.

"You will remember my child some of this when you wake. Your companions, who are your guides, wanted to take this opportunity and requested to meet you. Knowing about you and being present at the Haven when the gathering took place.

Brenna turned to the woman in white. Words were

not said; they were exchanged within.

"My sweet friend, I have been with you by your request before you came to this earthly realm. I have never left your side. We both have," as she nodded to the gentleman behind her. He nodded in agreement, *"as have my companions."* She patted their heads.

"When you feel relinquished, I bring you courage and strength, quickened from within."

Brenna smiled.

"We are always there for you." The spirit man spoke, *"I bring you peace and harmony, reconnecting you to nature. The God of us all adores us all. Opportunities sometimes can be masked by doubt. Nature will open your thoughts and allow you to continue with your journey."*

"What are your names, or do you have names?"

"We need not names in the ethereal; we do understand their necessity in the earthly.

"My name is Anise'. I come from the lost land of Atlantis."

"My name is Aru. I come from many lands, traveling the realm until we met in the ethereal. We knew our relationship would be one of harmony and enlightening the soul."

"We are aware the guide spoke to about your gathering. You must be aware many in the spirit are anxiously waiting to assist in any way they can. Though this task seems

unimaginable or inconceivable, remember you are designated as the creator, which is one who brings to be that which most cannot imagine."

~*~

The aroma of coffee filled the small cabin. Joe sat up and made sure Brenna was covered.

"She's fine, son, would you like a cup?"

"Yes, I would love a cup. She seems very peaceful. I'm pleased. We have a busy day ahead of us. This last year was very hard on her."

"Yes, it has been. Remember, everything always works out."

Joe smiled, knowing Mr. Henry was part of the whole plan too.

"The land you will be surveying today was chosen specifically for your production.

"Her sister will meet you at the Inn this morning. She is almost there.

"Your car has already been repaired and is waiting for you by the road."

Now Joe knew he was part of it.

~*~

Brenna walked with Joe to the car hand in hand. She was in deep thought.

"How did you sleep last night?" Brenna asked.

"I was a bit restless, just being aware of you and

sensing you weren't sleeping very well."

"I had a dream," or was it a dream, she thought. I think Henry took me for a walk last night. This person didn't appear as he looked here. I met two guides. They said they have been with me since I came to this world. Then he mentioned if I was familiar with the blending of the realms. Do you think Joe, Henry is a part of this somehow?" As she pointed around toward the trees.

He smiled, "That was an amazing dream, Bren. Aren't we all a part of this?"

"Yes, I understand. I think he plays a larger part in it. That's what I feel."

"He did say to me this morning while you were still asleep.

The land we're going to view was chosen for the production. That might be part of the blending of the realms he mentioned."

"I knew it!" She shouted. "I knew it! I bet if we walked back down that path. The cabin wouldn't even be there!"

"Do you want to? Do you have to go to the bathroom again?" He said with a smirk on his face.

Brenna smacked his arm. "That wasn't funny, Joe!"

He held back the laughter and focused on the drive toward civilization. Brenna kept checking her phone reception. Finally, she was able to call Laura.

~*~

"Where are you, Bren?

"Oh, you will get an ear full as soon as I see you!" Her Irish tongue was lashing out, and you could feel her energy.

"Henry said you were at the Inn, are you?"

"Who is Henry?"

Joe and Brenna laughed when she said that. "I will tell you later! We have a lot to share, and you won't believe it!"

"We checked in early this morning. The police told us you were safe. And a lady on a CB radio had contacted them. Communication here is a bit archaic, isn't it?"

"The Innkeeper at the Inn is very nice. He told Tim he had relatives not too far from here."

Brenna said, "Get yourself settled, and we will meet you there." There is a café here called the Novel Café. My god, I need a strong cup of coffee."

"You're kidding, right?"

"No, that's what it's called. I am looking at the sign right in front of me."

"Doesn't that name sound at all familiar, Bren?"

"Oh my gosh, from Gram's book!"

"Yes, I think we are walking back in time somehow. Check your calendar!" She laughed.

Joe's getting us a cup for the road. We have to

change and shower once we arrive. Then we will go together in one car.

Chapter Eleven

~~*

"What do you think?"
"Wait until they reach the location.
If they can feel comfortable and learn from this, then the next
step won't be so hard."
"I agree."

An elderly lady came out from the back kitchen.

"Welcome to the Novel café, my friends. What would your liking be, to begin your day?"

Remembering the story her grandmother wrote about the cafe, Bren asked. "Would you mind if I looked around your café?"

"Of course not, sweet girl. There is so much to discover here. Sometimes you have to have the eye to see it. Or you will just pass by--- then someone else will find it. The world is filled with unfound treasures."

Laura and Joe laughed so loud. "Where have we heard that before?"

"It's like we are in alternate universes, things mentioned and repeated, just in a different way."

"Yes, you're right."

"I have something for you; she handed Laura the envelope."

A smile came over her face while reading it. "Your mom promised me this when we first met. She talked to me about true love and how it comes to you in the most unusual ways."

She kept reading. "This is her dream."

"Yes, it is. It's from her journal about the first night she met Dad."

Laura held the paper up. "Joe, did you read this?"

"No."

"Joseph, where's that investigating reporter I have known and loved for years?"

He laughed.

Brenna took out the map that the town clerk gave her and set it on the table.

"Take a look at this."

"What is it?"

"Our mothers bought this section of land in October of last year."

"What?"

"Why?" Tim asked.

"I'm sure we will discover that very soon.

"Yes, as soon as we finish breakfast. I'm starving!" Joe said.

"Me too!" Tim agreed.

"Oh, you men always thinking of your stomachs." Bren laughed, and Laura agreed.

~*~

This time they took Tim's jeep. They were unanimous in leaving Brenna's Toyota at the Inn. The location, according to the map, was hard to understand.

"This entire area is nothing but trees and wildlife. The human population is non-existent. Maybe that's why Talise purchased it for privacy. I guess this is the road less traveled," Tim commented, keeping his eyes on the road to miss the potholes.

"Look, there's a marker."

Joe got out of the car. "It says turn around." He laughed.

"What?"

"The sign says:"

Turn around

Tim laughed," of course it does."

Now they were getting the idea of all of this: to follow the signs. They drove back at least two miles. Finally, noticing there was another sign.

Joe got out and read it and started laughing again.

"What? What does it say?" Brenna called out.

Now you're on the right path.
Take your next turn easterly.

Tim kept driving, waiting to see a turn. Suddenly, a huge moose came out of the bush.

"Oh my god, be careful!" Laura yelled. "Don't hit him."

"Hit him?" Tim yelled, "he would do more damage to my car than I would him. He's a giant."

"Here we go. There it is." Joe noticed a turn ahead.

When he turned, there was another sign.

"Welcome

TO IV PRODUCTION

They all cheered.

The building was hidden within the trees. They were all in awe of what they were seeing in front of them. The building was made of white stone with a huge engraved door in the front.

Men and women were working around the building, either planting or pulling foliage to make a clearing.

They waved as their car pulled in, almost as if they were expected.

There was a sign above the door that read

I.V. PRODUCTION

(Inspirational Village Incorporated)

A man came out the front door.

"Hello, welcome to I V production."

"Harry? Is that you?" Brenna asked as she approached him.

"It is you." Joe agreed. "What are you doing here?"

"I don't believe I have had the pleasure," Laura extended her hand.

"I am pleased to meet you, Miss Laura Lang. I have heard many things about you."

She smiled. "All good, I hope."

"Yes, of course."

Laura introduced Tim: "This is Timothy O'Farrell."

"Your family speaks highly of you,"

Tim thought. ("My family? How would he know my family, they all are dead?")

Henry heard what he thought very clearly. "Ahhh, Timothy, let not your eyes deceive you to what your heart knows is true. They are very, very much alive."

Tim was surprised.

He extended his hand to Joe. "Joseph, I apologize for your survival experience. It was to bring your sweet Brenna to me. We needed to get acquainted."

He patted him on the back. "I think you knew that, now didn't you?"

Joe smiled, "yes, sir."

~*~

"Follow me, please."

All four walked closely together, observing the surroundings.

Harry began to discuss what was going to transpire:

"You all have a great task ahead of you. A production such as this has never taken place.

"You've been made aware of your purpose with a limited glimpse of the Spirit world when you were at the Haven.

"This is going to be an awakening not just for you but for many in the earthly realm. The connection to the realm of Spirit has been minimal until now.

"Man has construed many theories that make one question theological moments. Yet, of course, many were misconstrued by men translating from one language to another. If one does have a connection to Spirit, they would decipher what was correct or man's imagination.

"To further engage men's minds, we *occasionally* allowed some to visit on a limited basis to share what exists in the world of Spirit. Many times, their words fell on deaf disbelieving ears.

"What you have been assigned to do will open the veil even broader than before. The divine purpose is to take the fear from the hearts of men and women. That has been planted within them to fear what is called death. We call it not death; nothing dies. They are coming home from where they parted to their life, their original life.

"The Council of elders, with permission, has put this into motion. Will it convince all? No, I am sad to share this. It shall not.

"While you're in your earthly body, you will not be able to view and comprehend the full expansiveness of our world. It is as vast and as omnipotent as the universe itself. This view and experiences that will take place in here will be giving all a glimmer."

~*~

"Let us begin if you are ready."
All acknowledge they were. Henry opened the grand door. The room was more extensive than it seemed from outside.

"Take a seat, and let's begin."

~*~

A soft mist came into the room, surrounding them like a cloud. It made them feel as if they were floating.

In the front of the room, a woman appeared and walked toward Joseph. She stood at a distance, knowing it would be a moment he would need to adjust to.

He began to stir, realizing his grandmother was standing before him. *"Hi, Joey."*

"Gram, I have missed you so much."

"I know, honey, it's a different process for us to be in touch with each other now. I tried to send you a sign at Maggie's with the pie. Do you remember?"

"Yes, I remember."

"That is how we or all of your loved ones let you know we are nearby. Oh, yes, there are other ways too."

A large group appeared behind her: All smiling and waving hello.

One spirit being said, *"yes, we do try!"*

Another called out... *"Sometimes, I'll flicker the lights to get my loved one's attention. At times it works; sometimes they think there is an electrical short,"* she laughed.

Another spirit being spoke: *"I make music play on the radio, and of course, the white feathers seemed to be more familiar now."*

Everyone laughed together; their laughter was like an angelic melody to their ears. Since the laughter was not of the vibration of the ear, it is of the heart.

"Oh my god. Look!" Tim said. "Mom?"

"Hi Timmy," she said. *"My sweet boy."*

Brenna and Laura knew this was a new experience for both men. The girls had learned and were familiar; their family was always nearby.

As the men stood, wanting to touch them. Laura and Brenna held their hands.

Names began being called out by both Joseph and Tim: "Grandpa, Aunt Beth. Look, there's my grandmother too. Oh my god, there's Stephen; he passed when I was twelve. Hi Stevie, you look the same. This is unbelievable." Tim cried as tears came down his face. Joe was just as emotional,

More and more appeared. The joy in the room was overwhelming, a true celebration.

"What's happening? How can this be?"

Suddenly a beautiful angel stepped from behind the gathering of the families.

All heard a melodic voice speak to them:

"Be at peace, dear ones. What you are feeling is how all feel when they transition. The joy of seeing loved ones greeting them as they come back home. They are all here for you and will be by your side as you continue your journey in the earthly. They know each of you has made an agreement to proceed with your life, and they all are so excited to watch it take place.

"This moment was orchestrated for you. To see it for yourself to be aware and teach others to comprehend. A teacher must learn first ... and so you shall.

"My name is Athena. I am an angel, as you can see."

She fluttered her wings.

"Your family members are all spirit beings. You refer to them as angels, but they are spirit beings. Here in this realm, there are many different forms, fairies, angels, spirit beings, ascended masters, archangels, spirit guides. You will become knowledgeable of them all as time proceeds.

"In our world, we are as the stars of the galaxy you abide within. Some lights are brighter in stature than others. Yet none is more glorious in the realm of Spirit than the other. We are the same.

"You see all your loved ones who have come back home. Which is here in Spirit. You will learn as time continues to call this HOME!" She elevated her voice.

"No one is being punished or treated with repentance. That is a human-made concept created in his mind. But know there is a dark side, one that gets pleasure within it.

This dark being does have a choice to stay within the dark or enter the light. You see just as in your earthly realm the saying on earth as it is in heaven is so very true.

"Each soul, as they came home, has an adjustment time. They still remembered their life, and some need to be counseled and consoled. They had to see life here was without pain and illness or domination. Whatever they wished for on the other side is possible here. Anything....

"Soon after their adjusting time, they are guided by others to create their homes and lives. Their deepest love is

carried on here. This is where yes; dreams do come true.

Martha, can you please explain to Joseph and share your experience with him."

She smiled… stepping closer to him. *"Hi, Joey--"*

He started to cry, hearing her voice.

"I have watched you for years. I have a new life now. We live in our own homes. There is no illness or infirmities.

"Look at me dance." As she spun around, "I can walk, I can dance.

"I know you remember how sick I was. You see me now aged as you remember me. But that was for then, honey. I had to appear to you like this, so you would recognize and know it was me.

Then she changed right before his eyes to a beautiful young woman glowing with life and shining.

"You're so happy, Gram!"

"Yes, Joey, I am. This is what it's like here.

"You were so sick at the end."

"I know that was my way to leave and come back home. It was a choice I made."

Brenna put her arms around Joe, knowing he was overwhelmed.

Athena stepped forward again.

"I understand your emotions are very high now. You have experienced the first stage of your learning.

Experience is the best teacher, as you are all aware. Through this, you will be able to accomplish so much more than you ever imagined.

"We will ask you to return tomorrow. Then the next stage can be shown.

"Will you?"

All acknowledged they would.

"Discuss this among yourselves tonight as you remember."

"We shall," Laura acknowledged.

Before their family faded, everyone stepped forward to spend a moment with their loved ones.

Laura smiled, seeing her mother, Vivian, and her grandmother. And, of course, Brenna saw Talise with Nathaniel. All bowed their heads and smiled.

"We will see you again. Watch for the signs."

"We will--" All said with tears in their eyes.

The room was as it was when they came in. All were back in their seats. The lights glowed with the twinkling of orbs soaring around the room, playfully dancing for them to enjoy.

It took a moment for them to get adjusted.

"Are you alright?" Henry asked. "Take your time," he calmed them, "take your time."

"Let's go out into the sunlight now," Henry guided them to the door.

Hours had passed in the time of earthly, but their experience seemed to be only moments.

He walked with them to the car.

"I will see you tomorrow," Henry said.

Joe stopped for a moment. "Will my Gram come again?"

"Not tomorrow, son. From this, you must take with you that she is always with you. What you experienced today is for you to learn she is alive, and there is a new way of sharing her love. You will hear her: just call her name, she will acknowledge she's there.

The love continues, the connections continue. The cord is never divided. When you transition, you will experience all that she and your family members are. It will be your time to return home."

There was total silence between them as they drove to the Inn. Twenty minutes into the ride, Tim says, "I have never even imagined anything like this was possible. It is an entirely new way of viewing things."

"Say what's on your mind, everyone." Brenna encouraged, "Clear it out. We know this isn't only about us.

"It will open the eyes of so many to what is precious here like we saw today.

"Being a part of this divine intervention is such an honor for us all. As many as possible need to have an awakening just as we needed it to."

Joe asked, "Do you think it will be as it was for us today for them?"

"Joe, I'm not sure; more will be explained tomorrow." Laura consoled him.

"It's time to blend the ways of the spiritual life to touch this earthly—the Blending of the realms." (I see now, Henry, I see. Brenna thought.)

Brenna continued: "They bring this understanding to make our life clearer and make many understand clearer. Taking away the fear.

"Many are terrified of heavenly or divine thinking because they feel it is a death that has to be when we leave our bodies.

"Let's relax and breathe. More will come tomorrow for us."

~*~

The Inn Keeper met them with a smile as all four walked into the sitting room area. "I understand your visit to the village was quite exciting." He smiled.

They all looked at each other and laughed loudly.

Tim dropped into the sofa with legs spread, taking a deep sigh. Joseph did the same.

Brenna suggested, "Let's go have a nice dinner by the water. I think they have a special on the lobster!"

~*~*~*

Chapter Twelve

The drive was easy this morning to reach the building hidden in the woods of Maine.

Henry was standing alone today. He could sense they were all anxious about what lesson there would be today.

"Today, we will continue for your clearer vision to understand. It will not be as personal as yesterday.
Are you ready?"

All acknowledged they were.

Joe's heart raced as he walked into the grand structure.

"It's alright," Brenna consoled him, reaching for his hand.

"Now please, will you all be seated."

As they did, a voice was heard, yet they saw no shape.

"Welcome, dear ones, in a moment you will see many

beings appear on the stage in front of you. There are also fairies and ministers of light, angels, spirit animals. The list can go on and on.

"We all abide within the Great Spirit of life. To which all live within whether in spirit or the corporeal. Nothing abides outside of the Great Spirit. Everything that exists comes from the substance of Pure Spirit. All life abides within. From the galaxies and undiscovered galaxies. All in all, even beyond your human comprehension.

"The inhabitants of the earth have acquired many remarkable findings and discoveries throughout the centuries. We will be putting those to use, not that we need it. Yet it will allow you and others not to question what they will be seeing. It is a technique available for their learning and understanding.

"It is time for your second lesson to begin. You will understand as best you can. You will then, without a doubt, in your heart, be able to understand the production and the creation of the village of inspiration since this is where the blending will occur for you and others."

"The village will calm corporeal hearts to understand they are not alone since most feel this often. They are not alone and never have been since the moment all decide to walk the earth plane.

"The experiences they have chosen at times lead them down a road that questions why they are there. Or events take place in their life, and they again ask the why of it.

We will open the veil of unanswered questions for them; to receive the answers from those that can clarify.

"I am requesting you pay attention to what I am about to share with you. Since it is knowledge, many in your time have not been taught this. In order for you to pass this to the seekers, you must genuinely be familiar and aware of what I am sharing.

Do you understand?

All acknowledged yes.

"Humanity has become so intelligent; they have lost the ability to disconnect from their physical life and become aware of the powers and nature surrounding them.

"The earth is thousands of years old. Some of you have come to the earthly realm many times. Of course, you do not remember what you accomplished or lived at that time. This is so your life before is not blended with your new journey.

"Allow me to share more with you---"

As he spoke, the stage filled with beings. Some more glorious than others. Some with wings and others not.

Lights flowed through the air, twinkling and then landing on a flower or a plant, changing into their fairy forms. They were lovely.

Animals began appearing lying down beside the

beings of light.

"The village will not be physical, as you know yours to be. It is an experience that will be offered and shared with the true seekers.

"We have here in this realm for the songwriter to be inspired to write more songs with the wonderfully talented artists.

"The painter to paint beyond what they feel possible.

"The authors write with confidence, being guided by the writers in spirit. It is a connection for as many that desire this to happen.

"It will make the unbelievable believable—all will be partaking in this new way of thinking and approaching life by the knowledge and understanding they will be given.

"Mothers and fathers who are needing guidance. They will be given advice.

"You see.... all is possible... when they unblock the doubts and emotions of unworthiness and impossibility.

"Their life will be enhanced now just for the asking. It is life changing for them for all.

"The village will be a ray of hope for the seekers. Not all will seek to be a part of it. Some will even try to replicate it for their financial gain. It is the way of man or some of them

to control and acquire power by manipulating others' minds. This has happened since the beginning of time.

"Would you like to see the village?

"Yes, of course, I know you are wondering how you will accomplish this. Since I say it isn't a physical location and it is real how can this be your asking. I will show you."

The room lit and lifted them all, so their view was looking down on the earth.

"There, do you see all the lights over there? Let's take a closer view, shall we?"

They soared above the treetops, where it was located, they were not sure.

The small cottage like homes were divided. Having a path that was flowing from the beginning to the end. Stones surrounding the village glowed from the energy given to them by the light.

A gazebo was in the middle of a flower-filled park in the center of town. (This looks familiar, Laura thought)

Four beautiful women appeared in front of them.

"We will guide you."

"Welcome to the village of Inspiration, dear ones. You were told of this moment at the Haven in Saol.

Now you will be able to see it visually.

You see, many locations here as they walked through the

village square; each has a unique experience for the seeker.

Here there are no divisions because of the colors of the skin. All within it live in harmony. All beliefs will understand the common core as unified in love.

Beings of all nationalities began appearing and walking within the village. Everyone was cordial and enjoying life.

Children were playing in the park; laughter was filling the air. Along with music playing in different locations.

There will be no control or domination, nor persecution allowed to exist. You see, in the midst there is an Eternal Flame. It is never extinguished. It is lit by the sun. It is the light of inspiration to all who come and abide here.

All will take from this place all they need as treasures within to their homelands. Each building does have inhabitants within them. Mothers, Fathers, spiritual leaders. Men of renown in the arts such as music, writing, historical buildings with your true history within the archives. It is filled with all you possibly could need or want.

"Many from the realm of spirit appear here from time to time to share their gifts. They all have a desire to inspire and guide each person as they come.

Once they experience the essence of the village, they need not be in a specific location once they depart. Since the learning and understanding will be within them. They are having a visual experience to that it is easily created within their life.

"They will learn and understand all they desire.

"There is a soothing of the soul council, an apothecary for those seeking medical assistance, not of man. Yes, this is to heal from within, then it will manifest without. This is a village, unlike any other. A truly heavenly experience created and made possible by your Heavenly Spirit Father and Mother.

"To be present here requires no financial necessities. Gifts should never require financial gain. The only requirement is needed are to listen and allow.

"The allowing is the most difficult since many humans have been convinced to have the blessings they wish for, it has to be earned. It does not."

They came back to their seats. It was like they never left.

"Let us give you all a moment to ponder. We ask that you stay on the property and absorb what you have been shown.

"Your notebooks are in your vehicle. Take a moment to sit and reexamine what you may need to. When you return, you may ask questions of us."

"This will be our final meeting, such as this. In the days ahead, you will know many are with you to guide and instruct.

"Ask and it is given, you need to remember this."

Henry walked with them to exit the building.

~*~

The afternoon sun was coming closer to the horizon. It took them a moment to adjust to the light.

Tables and a lovely spring was flowing on either side of the building. You could hear the rushing of water.

Laura walked towards the water. It was a small pond with a waterfall flowing into it. A pleasant surprise since the land was located in the middle of a wooded area.

Joe and Tim went to the car to retrieve everyone's tablets.

A small rabbit came out from under the bush.

"Hey, little one," Brenna said. The rabbit came right up to her as she sat on the grass with her hand extended.

Everyone settled at the picnic tables combining their questions, so they were unified. Answers were needed, and all that had been shown to them needed to be substantiated, so they knew what they were to do next. At the last gathering, the teachers told them that Brenna would be guiding.

This experience will be unlike anything that ever imagined. Yet each had their jobs.

They all agreed they had enough questions to understand what was to take place.

Henry sat on the stone-paved steps watching the four approach him.

They entered the building.

This time only one spirit being was present:

They all sat across from her as she began to explain in more detail.

"I have seen your questions....

Allow me to answer them for you."

She handed them a written booklet for them to read.

"I am going to ask you all to take turns reading this out loud now.

Brenna, you can begin:"

CLARITY

Keep this by your side. Remember, angels are in place to make the unbelievable believable.

Page 1

Many will approach you with a multitude of talents as soon as you return to your homes. They will come to you in unique ways.

You have already met one person before you left Saol. Mr. McGrath. He is a professional in holograms. This process will be one of many that will be used.

The other techniques will be revealed to you soon.

Brenna:

Your heritage goes back years at this time and before. All the women in your family have made the world aware of their presence in many ways. Writing, social work, lectures, guidance, the list goes on and on. All of those qualities abide within you and will be enhanced. This is why you have been designated as the creator and guide.

Laura:

You were taught by being taken under the wings of a master teacher. Talise Kavanaugh. In her short time with you, she took you from one realm to the next at a moment's notice.

Sometimes it was startling to you, and in it all, you understood and came away stronger. You are the dreamer making dreams come true. Are you the one that makes them come true? No, not actually, you are the guide to bring them to the experiences to see it is possible.

Just as Brenna is not the actual guide, she is the extension of the guide. She is not the creator but the extension of the creator.

Do you understand?

The documentary opened your eyes and those that partook in it—using visuals on the camera to putting things together piece by piece to present to the world.

Your place of employment isn't by mistake. It was chosen for you just as your mother and grandmother both partook in touching lives with the magazines and books they created. To their success, they were having the lives of others changed by them by their words. Hearing this, you can see how your life and Brenna's coincided and are similar to the other.

Page 2

Timothy:

You and Laura have had a powerful connection before this one in the realm of time in the 1700s.

Yes, I know this might stir you since you have no remembrance of this. The stories that were shared in the literature seeming to be fictional most assuredly were factual.

Your hearts have always been connected, and now they will be connected even stronger since it is true love that is the essence of all that will be taking place.

Joseph:

I am going to be bringing things to your attention now quite abruptly. I am sure you will understand. I am not creating your future experiences; I am making you aware of your past to bring you to now. Then things will be more apparent.

This isn't a one-time production. It is an experience for all, such as your videos and movies you have produced. Your place in all of this, with your knowledge and others, will be perfect.

You will see that since the beginning of time, the life you have led was to bring you to this moment.

You have chosen this as all do. We have no say in your decisions or choices. Yet, we will help and guide you through them. The ultimate intention of completion of the experience is entirely up to the participant. They can choose to continue or decide to come back home at their beckoned request.

Page 3

I am here to make you aware of all of this and how it came to be that you are all together. The experience you have seemingly been requested to do, you chose this before this time.

It isn't a challenging task. Your ego and material minds put up a block of concern to make it seem complicated. It is not.

The electronic age is dominant now. It also existed in another time, man misused it, and the experience had to be disconnected and eliminated. Then in time, it was brought back to start again.

This opening you will provide what is needed.

It will be a film production. For the seeker to enjoy as a movie-like format.

Page 4

You are all in wonderment since you see I am answering all your questions without them even being spoken. That is what takes place in our relationships.

It is time to calm your thoughts for you to see the doors will open, and talented people will be arriving both in the earthly and the ethereal realm. It will take place in "Inspirational Village." Many years ago, this name was by someone who wanted to create this, but the earthly moments were limited not to bring it to pass.

Remember, Deborah had her book written within her journals, and then as dreams never die, it is carried on. By her daughter, Leah finished it. As Brenna will complete her mother's vision of the Village of Inspiration.

That is the generational connection you have.

You see, dreams come true through the continuation of our children and their children. Dreams never die. They are very, very much alive.

You must remember that if someone dreams a

dream, it will enhance all life. It will continue in the realm of time, maybe years, maybe generations later, but it will continue.

"Please set your booklets on your lap and listen to my words.

"Our time, I do feel it has allowed you all to see this with clarity. Do not make things complicated when they are the energy of life will not flow smoothly through it.

"All of you will continue to live your life and create new dreams to experience or to put the call out to the universe to come to a place at a later time.

"We are all here; you have seen this in your gatherings in your little town of Saol. Great things can come from little moments when you believe they can."

She sent a breeze through the room, then they all appeared back by the lighthouse.

Joe commented. "I have had that experience before with Talise. I think we need to relax and enjoy this time with the water. We all have an idea of what this grand experience is to be. Right?"

Brenna laid her head on the grass. Holding the

booklet, she had been given. "Yes, I do, this is spectacular."

Chapter Thirteen

Back in Saol, Maggie walked to Shamans Cove to visit with Allura. She smiled as the wind chimes played their tune. "Allura, are you here?"

When there was no response, she went to the back area of the store. "Allura? Are you busy?"

Looking out the balcony glass door, she could see her leaning on the rail, as if in deep thought. Maggie tapped on the window and opened the sliding glass door. "Hey, my friend. Are you alright?"

"Hi, Mag-- Yes, I'm fine. I just wanted to come out and look at our beautiful lake. I need to do this more often. Life seems to be so busy lately."

"I agree-- Maybe we should take a trip somewhere together. We haven't done that in years."

Allura laughed. "No, we haven't. We should consider this. We aren't as young either."

"Great, then all the more reason to do it. Our staff can handle everything."

"Did you have a place in mind?

"Let's have a cup of tea and see what our old minds can snap up. Shall we?"

~*~

They both have lived in Saol now for almost 60 years. Things have definitely changed since they first arrived.

"Have you heard from the girls lately?" Maggie inquired.

"Not lately. Laura and Tim were in a rush last week. Something about going to Maine to rescue Brenna. I heard that from Grace at the Haven. She has quite an imagination explaining things."

Maggie laughed, "rescue aye? More like go investigate, you know how Laura has that reporter in her genetics, it just makes her blood flow."

As they both eased into the moment, they could sense the presence of someone.

"Come out, come out where ever you are or whoever you are," teased Maggie.

The soft voice laughed, *"I could never get anything by you, could I?"*

"No, you couldn't, neither in the body or out. That's the fun of it all. Right?"

"Right." Talise agreed.

"So, fill us in, madam beholder, what's new in the realm of no rules, no time."

We are keeping ourselves busy. Our home is lovely, and Nathaniel has decided to take up gardening. It's not a difficult task; you think it, and you create it. You have to be clear and make sure it is precisely what you want".

"Do you see others from your family often?" Allura asked.

"Oh, my goodness, there is so much to tell you. It's more beautiful than anyone can comprehend. We can soar above the land and see the waterfalls and all the animals enjoying life. Food isn't necessary there, so there is no threat to the animals. The food chain doesn't exist in the ethereal."

"I'm sure the food pyramid doesn't either," Allura joked.

They all laughed as Talise sat at the table with them.

"The easiest way to say it, it is about love. It has all the things the earthly has without the negative within it. Yes, we can soar above the earthly too. It is so much fun!

"My mother appears from time to time if I call to her. She is a young 30yr old playing and dancing. Most chose to go to that age appearance. When we appear to you in the earthly, we appear as you remember us."

"Is it hard to envision all this?" Talise asked. *"To have a life with absolutely no negative, I think it would be hard to understand.*

"*But let's talk about why I am here.*

"*We felt since you are the elders closest here for the girls, to give you a wee bit of foresight to guide the girls if they need to be guided. We, of course, will be doing that as well.*

"Of course, we both understand," Allura replied.

"*Good. The Council felt I should come to prepare you.*"

"*All the lightworkers are on the alert and ready to assist the girls in their production. Soon they'll be returning home.*

"*Now, to be clear, we've never spoken to the girls on the dark side. It will be the next educational lesson for them, since how can they guide others if they know not of it themselves.*"

"I see," Maggie said. "What should we do to help?"

"*First, many will be appearing to help with this production of Inspirational Village. The discernment of the volunteer's nature will need to be activated by them.*

"*Of course, the dark will never have power over the light when all is said and done. The darkness will make some beings have a difficult time to decipher between the two.*"

"*Allow me to share this with you: She opened her hand, and a device was there. Let's go inside. You will see a lightworker sharing her view of what is taking place.*"

~*~

The room they were in, filled with light. A woman appeared as if a vision. Behind her and around, you could see buildings and movement of life.

~*~

Her voice quivered, knowing her time was short to share this:

"My name is not necessary since I am only here for a short time. Where I come from, names aren't necessary. We know each other from the light energy we share. I am here to warn and make aware to the Lightworkers and guides here in the earthly.

"Be watchful, my dear ones. There is a darkness on the land. Not of a physical, it is of an encompassing emotional essence. This darkness to whom we do know the source. It is taking away hopes and dreams. It is very conniving, and if I close my eyes and listen and sense, it is as a shadow: a faint shadow that isn't covering the sunlight, but the light from within.

"The dark is capable of hiding what most thought was real and everlasting in this realm. They (*because there are many*) are distracting many souls from their life force so that it is challenging to enliven their souls.

"It's taking over this realm. I am wondering, as I share this, was it always there? Yes, I genuinely do think so. I wasn't in tune with it, as many that abide here are not or were not.

"I feel it is a lower, but compelling energy. It kept pulling me deeper and deeper. It was trying to entangle the light I had within to become a part of the dark.

"I know I am a teacher and a guide; I must go to where this takes me. Within it, I saw many struggling with right and wrong, truth and lies, hope, and hopelessness.

"I would reach out my hand to many, yet the darkness blinded them. They couldn't see my hand! So, I had to get closer and touch them. As I did, I sensed my energy going within them.

"Days turned to weeks and months. My power was waning, so very low. Many were told not to speak, be still, and listen to what the leaders are saying—telling them with social networking and news channels that they knew what's best for them.

"I knew this was not true, yet I stayed with the voiceless, having my voice of my soul scream out to them. Stay awake; don't be lulled to sleep. They want to control you to take away your livelihood. There are thousands upon thousands. My two hands could only reach so many.

"This is like a plague of sadness of a nothing that takes away everything. Everything that is loved, everything that is joyful. My heart is aching.

"My guide came to me and whispered in my ear:"

"You are in it but not of it. Step back; one being saved is as precious as a thousand. Others are doing the same all over the world. My sweet girl, step out of it so you can see."

"I listened:

"Who is their hero going to be? Will Father come to bring them home? I asked."

"All is going to be fine. Trust in the Divine, and **know** this is only for a season.

We will not let you slip again. Though you needed to realize each soul is destined for what it chooses.

Do you see?"

"Yes, I said, this is not where I belong.

"As I spoke, a beam of light came from heaven and surrounded my body. I was being lifted; I could hear the cries of the people. Is this the land of torment? I said to my guide."

"To some, it is but not to all. The darkness takes those who are willing to be taken."

The light transported her to the trees in a meadow by a stream. "This is yours and their safe place, away from the buildings of concrete. The darkness has no power over nature. It is the life of the planet. Into nature is where you, my child, lead them to. Call to them from here. Go not into their battleground. The nothing is very authoritarian out there.

"Here is where the voice is heard and not covered by cloaks of men. Here is where your breath is free, and joy experienced.

"Walk the land. There are others here. You are not alone. As you heard the cries, you will hear the laughter. Go always towards the melody of joy and love. There is your peace, sweet girl.

"What is taking place will not interfere with your life. What surrounds you is a higher vibration. Many will be in the darkness and pulled from it. When they ask to be.... "

At the end of the vision, the woman stood silent, staring into what seemed to be a camera. The wind was blowing through her hair, and tears were flowing down her cheek.

"Please stay awake. You'll find your way. Listen to the call of nature, and there you will find what your heart has always desired. We are waiting for you with open arms."

Both were quiet and stirred, watching the video.

Talise said, *"I will be here for you as all in the spirit*

world are. This is being shared with you, so you are forewarned. Not all are of the light, and they will try to maneuver into the production. You know what to do. You have lived in this realm and understand the ability of darkness to make itself appear as light."

Maggie spoke first. "I have a clear vision, and you need not worry about the girls."

"We will surround them with light and understanding," Allura said.

Chapter Fourteen

Maggie and Allura walked toward the cafe.

"So much for a trip, aye Allura?" Maggie laughed.

"I think this will require our presence in other areas, Maggie. We already said our staff could handle things.

"Yes, we did."

The door to The Journey swung out quickly. It was Mr. McGrath leaving. "Oh, excuse me, ladies." Almost bumping into them.

"No problem, Mr. McGrath. I hope you enjoyed your dinner."

"I did, I always have. My Sara knew what she was doing finding this little town."

"Mr. McGrath," Maggie said. "Do you mind if I ask you a question?"

"Of course not."

"When you first arrived, I found your name was very familiar. I just remembered why? Do you have any relatives in Boston?"

"Yes, I guess I do. My sister's boy moved there when

he finished college. I think he's working at WWSE television station."

"Would his name be Joe?"

The surprise on his face was evident. "Yes, it is."

Maggie tapped Allura's arm. "This is our Joseph's uncle."

"Our Joseph?" Mr. McGrath said.

"It seems your lovely wife Sara had more of a surprise for you here in Saol. More than just your pie, you loved."

"If you have time, would you like to come back in? I would like to share something with you. I'll get you another piece of pie, too!" She laughed.

~*~

The foursome were a few miles out of town. The drive back to Saol felt as if they were coming home.

"Let's stop at The Journey. It's only a couple of miles up the road. I'm starving."

"Me too." Tim agreed.

Joe and Brenna were directly behind them.

Both cars pulled into the last two spaces in front of the cafe. Laura said, "Thank you."

The door flew open, and Shadow ran straight for Laura. "Oh my gosh, boy--"

"Hey, boy, where's Maggie?"

"Where do ya think I would be out milkin the cows?" Maggie called out from the open door.

"Get in here. We missed you and are so pleased your home. It's much sooner than we expected."

All the locals in the restaurant were aware of what Brenna and Laura had been doing. Everyone applauded as they came in.

"How did it go?" One customer called out.

The surprised look on their faces was evident.

"Is the village coming to life now?" Another called out.

Brenna smiled: "It will be soon. How did you know what we were doing?"

Allura explained, "In this little village, news travels fast. Everyone has viewed the village on their tables since your mother painted it. So many would ask where it was? Your mother would say it will appear in time, within each one of your lives. Be patient."

They moved to a larger table so everyone could have something to eat. Brenna helped Mr. McGrath carry his pie and coffee.

"Umm, this looks good," she said to him. "I see you are friends with our sweet ladies. My name is Brenna Kavanaugh. It is so nice to meet you."

"I met Laura about a week ago. I am Mr. McGrath."

She was surprised to hear his name. "Mr. McGrath?"

"Yes, Joseph McGrath."

She smiled, "I think I have someone you might like to meet. Joe, she called out. Could you come over here for a moment?"

He walked around the table. "Yes?"

"Joe McGrath, I would like you to meet Joseph McGrath."

They both were surprised.

"Really?" Joe said

"Yes, son, I'm your uncle. I was just as surprised as you when Maggie and Allura told me you were here too."

"Sir, it is very nice to meet you."

They had a lot to share and would
have more than enough time.

Maggie shared with Joe how his uncle came to the village. Everyone was not surprised.

"What is your profession?" Brenna asked.

"I guess you could say I have been an adventurer since my precious wife Sara passed a few years ago.

"She always loved following Talise and her presentations. Saol was the last place we came for a visit. Lake Aisling was her happy place. During our forty years together, I was a production overseer for movies. Specifically, in holographs. I loved it."

All four gave surprised glances to each other.

Brenna smiled: "Now it begins."

"Mr. McGrath, it's such a pleasure to meet you. If you have the time tomorrow, we would love to talk with you about a project we are orchestrating."

"I would love to. It seems all I have is time, so this would be most enjoyable."

Joe sat down next to his uncle. He could feel his mother was in the room too. (Okay, mom. Okay)

~*~

First thing in the morning, Laura called her boss in Boston.

(The world as we see it: WWSI television station.)

The phone rang. "Hello WWSI, how may I direct your call?"

"This is Laura Lang. Can I speak to Tom?"

"Sure, Miss Lang, one moment please."

"Hello, this is Tom." (His voice sounded different)

"Tom, this is Laura, are you alright?"

"I am, he said, but the world outside is not."

"What are you talking about?"

"Haven't you watched the news lately?"

"No, I was in Maine getting things ready for the

production."

"Ahh, yes, I see. Come back to earth, my co-producer. Turn on your television and connect with what's taking place. It's not a pretty sight.

"Give me a call back in an hour. I will be in the office.

"This call connected you to my cell phone. I'm covering a story in the downtown area with the camera crew."

"Alright, I will."

~*~

"Tim, come quickly; we have to turn on the news." She called Brenna and Joe. "I think we need to watch this together. I know the cabin has no television, so come to the Haven as soon as you can."

The television shared disturbing news.

Not just for Boston, the entire nation.

"What's happening out there?" Brenna said.

"It looks like a rebellion of sorts. But why, what is engaging this."

Maggie and Allura came through the front door. Knowing this would be unsettling for them.

Laura pointed to the television--- "Maggie, what's happening?"

"We will explain. It was important to get you home before you were made aware of the chaos and disruption."

Tim made a call to his company too: "My god, my staff is half staffed right now. What the hell is going on?"

Maggie asked everyone to be seated, "We will explain."

Mr. McGrath was staying at the Bed and Breakfast not far up the road. He saw all the cars parked at the Haven and pulled in the driveway; he knocked on the door. Opening it slowly, he called out, "Can I come in, please?"

"Of course, you can. You need to hear this too.

"The world is going through an adjustment. It started with a virus. Now the virus has turned inward to effect man's mind and their judgment.

"It seems overwhelming, and I assure you all is in hand."

"Is this because of the?" --- Brenna asked.

Allura said instantly--- "yes!"

"There is a dark nature that has always abided in the earthly realm.

"Each kingdom, plant, animal, water, air, and man are all being affected. The dark is trying to overtake them with tremendous power.

"Talise came to inform us two days ago about what was taking place. We thought it would be a while before it happened. It wasn't. It appeared within days. Once the darkness is revealed, it is energized even more potent by the sources it pulls into it.

"The dark power cannot overcome the intensity of the light. They always have co-existed in different kingdoms. You, my sweet girls, have never been guided in understanding and discernment of the dark. Your next lesson, as in all lessons, you must experience them first hand."

Brenna added, "Yes, mom always said that experience was the best teacher."

"She is correct"-

A voice from within the room spoke out.

Two beings of elegance and light appeared.

~*~

"I am Michael, and this is Raphael. We have felt your concerns and are being sent here to give you peace and understanding. All is as it should be both in the ethereal and in the world of the human form.

"Please, disconnect the mechanical viewer so you can hear our voices with no disruption."

Joe turned the television off.

"What's taking place and will be taking place for a short time. It is a struggle between dark and light. There has

always been a contention. Your interpretation as it takes place to who is stronger or weaker is in the eyes of your soul. Your sides will be chosen.

"You were not aware of this because you were sheltered by your parents and their power and energy. You are still protected, be wise in your choices and selections.

"You need to discern now that you are enlightened. Whenever in doubt, sit with your elders to guide you in this realm and ours. Do not be afraid you have the shields of a thousand angels. You don't see them, but they are there."

Brenna stood:

"We are honored by your presence. Thank you for assuring us with the words you are sharing.

"May I ask--- is this experience going to lengthen the time it will take to organize the production of the Village of Inspiration?"

Raphael spoke:

He nodded, acknowledging her and her inquiry.

"Sweet one, all is as planned. The darkness will never hinder the creation that will be taking place by the light. It is trying to block those that would seek this from coming forth. Those that are to experience will be successful in their journey.

"You will be selecting many to assist and, as in all things

negative, will attempt to blend in as light.

"If one is filled with dark, you will sense this immediately and some after only a short time. They intend to take the treasure and use it to their advantage.

"You will know. You have each other to converse with."

As he finished, many beings from the spirit realm appeared—an overwhelming moment for Mr. McGrath to see. The clarity was given to him so quickly. When he saw his beloved Sara standing beside the beings of light. His tears flowed down his face.

Allura held his hand to comfort him.

"This new experience that is coming to inspire with authentic engagement has indeed angered the dark. Their cover of deception will be revealed.

"You, my sweet girls, will show the seekers guidance not to fear.

"We are the messengers of the true light. They of the dark have their boundaries and are very aware of them. They are not allowed to touch you further than your first level. You will soon understand the good in it all."

Laura asked--- "Sir, what do you mean by the first level?"

Michael answered:

"Many you see standing here beside me have partaken in the earthly human form. Their first level had been compromised in one way or another. But their heart and spirit were strong to bring them through it. Some decided to come home. They knew their experience in the earthly had been completed as they chose before they arrived.

"We do not make the choices for them; we are always with them either way they chose. To give strength and comfort or to have our hand there if they reach out to us to come home.

Now we will leave you to begin your journeys."

The room filled with a bright light, and they were gone.

All had experienced this before; it was a first for Mr. McGrath. He sat so still in his chair. Brenna was concerned for him. "Are you alright, Joseph?"

His eyes lit up, "yes, my dear, I'm alright."

He took a deep breath. "I saw her--- I saw my Sara!! Everything she tried to make me understand was true. It was true! Life does continue! He shouted. "It does continue!"

Everyone in the room was so pleased for him and celebrated his new awakening.

"Does anyone want some breakfast?" Maggie called out.

"I'm starved," Tom called out, and so did Joe.

"Me too," Mr. McGrath agreed. "I think I'm going to be here for quite some time."

Everyone laughed: "Yes, you are sweet, man," Brenna said. "Yes, you are."

~*~*~*~

Chapter Fifteen

Laura went outside and called Tom, her boss. He updated her on all that was taking place in Boston. His concern was when she and Joe would be returning.

"This is a circus out there," Tom said. "I don't know when it will settle down. It's like this energy has taken over people's minds."

(This was truer than he even could realize)

Laura didn't know how she would explain this to Tom but knew she had to try. "I will be back by Monday, and then we can talk."

Returning inside the Haven, Tom was standing watching the television—clicking it from one channel to another. "My god, Laura, look at this."

Towns were burning, and businesses were being destroyed. "Where is the protection from the government with so many towns being under attack?"

"How is your building?" She asked.

"It's standing many of my employees live outside of town. Those I have spoken to say it is mostly happening in the larger cities."

"It is an uprising without a doubt." Laura's voice was concerned. "We can't be distracted by this. We need to complete the production even if chaos is surrounding us. Remember what we were told."

"I know, I know, this is my livelihood and others too.

"Yes, but as Michael said, we can be touched on the *first level*. Remember? The first level is what this is. It's what is happening. Or with our health. We will make it through this. Please try to keep your eyes on the other side of the storm.

"I know good does come from the bad. In some ways, it is waking people up. Everyone is always rushing here and there, not taking time to enjoy life and being alive. They have even put that same energy now into their children.

"People don't communicate with each other face to face. It has to be with a cell phone or computer.

"Remember all the times you were in the airports? No one talked to each other. The mechanisms of man have taken over. So, it had to be adjusted. I see what is taking place. Similar to a re-set button.

"More people are home now with their families, seeing what is essential. This experience is like a rushing tornado, and all are in their homes to be safe.

"I'm sure many of your employees have found they can do work from home on their computers. Right?"

"Yes, I guess so." Tim acknowledged.

Laura knew how to calm him. "I'm driving to the cabin now--- Do you want to come?"

"Sure. I need to relax and focus my energy too."

~*~

Tim could feel his heart calming as they came closer to the cabin. Laura reached across the seat and held his hand.

He smiled at her. "Being with you has changed my life."

Laura smiled at his sweet confession, "I love you too, sweet Tim. My Mr. Forget me not."

Brenna was making her and Joe a cup of tea.

"This is amazing. What did you put in it?"

"Oh, just a wee bit of this and that," she laughed. (Brenna had learned the art of the apothecary in Ireland and was very creative in her creations. Whether medicinal or healthy alternatives.)

Shadow had been staying with Brenna since Laura was at the Haven. He started jumping around, trying to get out the front door.

"What's up, boy?" She heard a car pulling into the driveway. We have company."

Tim and Laura walked hand in hand towards the cabin. Shadow greeted them with his familiar jovial self.

Laura remembered her and Joe's first time here. (Meeting Talise as she sat by the water. So many questions were going to be answered by this incredible woman. Questions: she didn't even realize she had. She thought it was for an interview, but there was more for her to learn as life had taken charge. Thinking back, it seemed it was a lifetime ago.)

Joe touched her hand, knowing she was looking back. "She did change our world, didn't she? She told us she would, and we would get much more out of our connection than just a documentary on her.

"Do you remember when we were in the car on the way here? We listened to her recorded lectures. We both laughed, thinking she was a crazy old lady out here in nowhere land."

"I miss her," Laura agreed. "I miss seeing her sweet face and her gray hair blowing in the wind. Remember her jacket? I wonder where that is? She said she would tell me where she got it?"

Brenna spoke up. "I have it, and I know the story.

My great-great-grandmother wore it."

"Really? Then it was years old."

"Yes, it was. But it never aged. It would be a special memory to never age and passed on from generation to generation."

"Would that mean it was Debra's?" Joe asked.

Brenna smiled; "do you remember the story of her meeting my grandfather on the boat?"

"Yes," Laura said… "he put it over her shoulders to keep her warm on the sailboat."

"Exactly."

"I thought that was a dream?" Laura said.

"Was it?" Brenna snickered.

Both stood there, amazed at what they were hearing. Joe's mind was thinking back to the story as he stared at the water.

"He asked her to marry him under the full moon on the boat," Joe said from his memory.

Tim listened since he was also familiar with the story from his grandfather.

"Not everything is as it seems sometimes, is it? All our lives, all the moments from our families have brought us to this."

~*~

(Each of their lives had things to be attended to. They were aware their separate worlds needed some adjustments.

Brenna: She was being guided to complete her business in Ireland. It wouldn't be difficult, since her coming back to the United States, a dear friend was running her Apothecary. Now a new life was being shown to her, one that she had dreamt of for years. Now it was coming alive.

Laura: Was co-producer of the television station WWSI. Was she to walk away from it? Her mind struggled with that decision. She had loved the interaction with the world, broadcasting the truth that was not present in many news media venues, whether in print or in the television format.
Her decision would come in time. For now, she felt the necessity to keep her roots in Boston.

Joe: Worked beside Laura for years. He was finding his way in life, being a bit younger than she. His camera followed her, where ever the story led them. It was the first time he felt he was making a difference in the world. The satisfaction of each documentary they created was the first time he thought he was touching the world. Right now, he would need to make some choices that he never anticipated occurring. But then that is how life is. It brings you gifts you never believed possible. Right now, her name was Brenna.

Tim: His life took an unfamiliar, unexpected direction.
A dream that was shared with him at the beginning of Laura's letter discovery. In an old desk in his office building. He, too, had to make some choices. What he was to do for his next direction, he had to be patient and see.)

The foursome decided to relax for a time in Saol.

"Tonight, is Harvest Moon!!!" Brenna shouted.

"Oh my gosh-- I didn't realize it. Everything has been so busy, I almost forgot."

"We need to call Maggie and see what's happening in town tonight. Why hasn't anyone said anything to us?" Laura wondered.

Brenna took Laura by the hand. "Come with me."

They walked beside the water with Shadow by their side as always.

The guys just looked at each other and smiled.

"Would you like a brew?" Joe asked Tim.

"Now you're speaking my language."

The time passed relatively quickly, with the girls laughing and talking together like two sisters sharing life and enjoying every moment of their being together.

~~*

"They remind me of us, aye, Vivian?"

"Yes, they do!"

"Did you see the little ones who are preparing to come to be with them yet?"

"Yes, I did. Let's go see them so we can tell them what their Mommas are up to."

Everyone got in their vehicles to head to Saol.

They were surprised when they entered the village. It was very quiet. An unsettling calmness was present.

Laura was the first to enter The Journey. "Where is everyone?" She called out.

Maggie came out of the kitchen as her sweet jovial self. "What love were you expecting a parade or banners hanging. Maybe a party of some sort."

"No... it's just that usually, the town is buzzing with Harvest Moon coming tonight."

"Give it some time. The townspeople are being cautious since all the protesters have taken over the larger cities, not wanting to draw attention here. We have done our best to make it safe for all who come. Always remember the saying less is more will be our motto until things settle out there.

"We all will be gathering at the lake tonight around 8 pm. There will be local music and a large bonfire with, yes, tantalizing food from yours truly and other locals."

"I like the sounds of that," Brenna said.

"Come on, we have some time until it begins. Shall we go for a drive?" Tim suggested. "Then come back for a bite to eat?"

Laura agreed that was a great idea.

"I think I am going to take my girl for a walk in the woods," Joe said. "Everything has been so busy for her. I think she needs a bit of grounding."

"Grounding?" Laura asked, "what is grounding?"

"It's another process I learned about while studying with her at the cabin. You did know Brenna had a health store in Ireland, didn't you?"

She smiled, listening to Joe's sharing of life with them. He had paid attention.

He continued: "Grounding is connecting to the earth. Walking and having the energy that is within the earth enliven you."

"Oh, like hugging a tree," Tim jested.

"You can show your sarcasm, but yes, that too."

"If you stand beside a tree and lean on it. The energy from the tree brings health to your body. I know most aren't aware of this. Remember, this is all part of the awakening taking place out there for quite some time now.

"Remember, nature is the one area the humans can't hide from us. It's where we go to get answers and be calm. That's why Talise always went for walks and went by the water."

Maggie chuckled. "You have paid attention, Joseph. I am so pleased."

He had a smug smile on his face; it felt good to be

the teacher after most of his experiences were always being the student.

"Are you ready?" He said to Brenna.

"Of course, I can't think of anything nicer to do. Except we won't run into any dogs and old men, right?"

He laughed. "No, I think you're safe in making that assumption."

The day went very smoothly, all in their ways aligned to what would be coming to pass.

~*~

The bonfire was glowing under the star-filled sky. The moon reflected its essence on the lake of dreams. Hundreds of villagers gathered to celebrate the harvest moon. It was a joyful moment for them all. The music played, some danced, some just sat in their chairs watching and taking it all in.

Allura approached Joe: "Joe, I have a gift given to me by Talise last year. I think it would be perfect for you to give it to Brenna. Talise wanted her to have it on the first Harvest moon after she transitioned.

"Would you mind?"

The box was small, covered with velvet.

"Of course, I will." He put it in his pocket, waiting for the perfect time to give it to Brenna.

He watched her from a distance. Her smile on her

face and the joy radiated around her. As she and a group of women held hands dancing around the fire. It was a view one rarely sees. Yet you could feel the magic in the air. I wish I could keep that smile on her face, he thought.

You can.

The voice within told him.

You can.

Brenna saw Joe watching her. She ran to him, taking him by the hand to dance with her.

The song changed to "Harvest moon," he sang the lyrics to her as he held her close.

When we were strangers, I watched you from afar. When we were lovers, I loved you with all my heart. But now it's getting late, and the moon is climbing high. I want to celebrate see it shining in your eyes.

She began to cry, hearing him sing to her. "I love you, Joey."

"I love you too, my sweet Brenna. Will you marry me so we can dance at every harvest moon for the rest of our time here?"

"Yes, yes, I will," she squealed with joy.

Then he pulled out a box, not the one from her mother but from him. He placed the ring gently on her finger.

Joe called out to the crowd. "Can I have your

attention, everyone? This wonderful woman has agreed to share her life with me." Brenna raised her hand, and everyone cheered.

Such a magical celebration.

(Brenna was wearing the coat her great-great-grandmother wore when Robert proposed to her.)

~~*

Debra and her Scotsman smiled.

"That coat still has the magic, doesn't it love?"

"The magic is the wearer angel."

There was still more to the night, yet the joy of two in love made this moment one to remember.

"I have a gift for you, love, from your mom. Allura gave it to me and asked me to give it to you."

"Really?"

"Yes, she wanted you to have it on the first Harvest moon after she stepped into Spirit."

He opened the box. It was a beautiful silver necklace with a lovely delicate crystal full moon. The engraving said: Remember, I am always near my precious daughter.

Joe placed it on her neck as the tears flowed.

~*~*~*

Chapter Sixteen

It didn't take long for the news to hit the airwaves. Talents from all over the world appeared to share in their enthusiasm to assist.

Brenna stayed in the village, putting some things together and making some phone calls to Ireland. She was going to be married soon, and her life would need to be adjusted. She was aware of the time difference yet still knew her partner would take her call.

"Rachel, hi. I am so sorry for the timing of my call."

"Ahh, my friend, it tis grand to er yer lovely voice. Ya know we aven't allowed time to interfere with us. Aye?"

Brenna laughed. "Tis true tis very true. So much to talk about, my friend. First, before I get to my journey, how are you? Is all well with your family?"

"We are doin fine, a wee bit of discontent out in our

world. But I see you ave this too. The apothecary is fine. The business has grown lately, mostly for herbal tinctures to calm people. It is very stressful.

"What are your thoughts on all of this, Brenn?

"I know you are able to view life a wee bit clearer. I was just wondering what you're seeing."

Brenna took a moment to have the right words to share. "It is just for a time all that is taking place. Try to keep yourself and others as uninvolved as possible. It will pass within a few months. We all need to be patient."

"I understand and know there is more to this than what you're sharin. I can hear it in your voice. I know an ocean divides us right now, but our hearts ave always been connected. When you didn't come home sooner, I knew there was a situation that was taking place to make your time away longer."

"Yes, so much has happened. Mom took her journey to Spirit last year, as you know. She left me with many responsibilities, and I'm handling them as best I can.

"I won't be returning now for quite some time. But I will come next year, if only for a visit, to introduce you to my fiancée."

"What?? Your fiancée? Oh, my lass tis a lovely

moment you have shared with me. I am so pleased!"

"I am too. It just happened. It happened so quickly

our connection is a wonderment, to be sure. I will be taking care of all my obligations over there when I return.

I would like to ask you before I come if you and your lovely daughter would like to be the new proprietors of the apothecary?"

"Of course, we would!"

"Wonderful, I will keep the finances flowing if they are needed until we sign the final agreements when I come. If that is agreeable with you?"

"It is... when do you think you might be comin?"

"I am not sure I wanted to make sure you were well and would accept my offer.

"Of course, the apartment above will be available for you to live in too."

"Brenna, you have taken concern from my heart. I had no idea how my life would continue without working and doing what I love."

"I understand. Always know that fear and concern can be taken away. Now get some sleep if you can. I will be there soon enough, love."

~*~

The others were on their way to Boston. Two of them to check on their homes and one to make arrangements to pack and relocate back to Lake Aisling.

When they entered Boston, it was quiet and still recognizable. By the news channels, it made it seem the town was being destroyed. There were signs of disruption, but it still felt like home to them for the most part. They stopped at their regular coffee shop to try to adjust to being back. It had been a while, and so much had taken place.

The owner of their regular coffee shop recognized them. "Welcome back strangers!"

"Thank you," Laura said. "I hear the natives are restless lately."

He laughed, "yes, it seems to be occurring more and more, mostly at night. They like to use the dark to conceal their faces. They have caused an uproar, not just here but all over.

"Groups are fighting for government control issues to health concerns, and some are only looking for a fight. One seems to be replaced daily by another. There aren't too many happy people out there.

"Many of the locals stayed close to home. Some of these rioters are being transported here on buses by some in high financial power. They are trying to cause chaos to bring their agenda to the surface."

"I 'll meet you at the office in an hour, Joe. Okay?"

"Yes, I am going to drive by my apartment and check things out."

"Me too," Tim said. "I'll meet you there as soon as I

can. I have to check on my building and go pick up Charlie."

~*~

Laura took a moment to drive around and see for herself. Some of the buildings in the center of town had smashed windows. Cars blackened by fire were on main and side streets. People were camped in tents, all over some in front of some of the most prestigious buildings in Boston.

She couldn't believe her eyes.

(Don't get pulled into it: Rise above it.)

Turning the corner, it seemed normal. Her street and others were fine. The one thing she did notice, no children were playing. Where were the children? It seemed as if she was walking into a bad dream.

A car horn beeped behind her. Its lights were flashing. It was Joe.

They pulled to the curb.

"Are you alright?"

"I think I'm in shock."

"Me too," he said. "Did you drive by the park?"

"No, what's there?"

"Tents, hundreds of tents. I didn't see people; I think they were all sleeping in them. These must be the outsiders that were sent here."

"Oh my god, Joe. Our home is being invaded and destroyed."

Then Tim pulled up behind them. Charlie was in the back seat. He was highly energized.

"Stay, boy," Tim said as he got out of the car. The look on his face was anger and disbelief.

Laura ran to him. "I'm here," she said. "We're going to be fine."

He needed to see her, to touch her. "Laura, it's gone.... My building is destroyed. I called my staff, and everyone is terrified. I have 25 employees. They all are working from home. I'm not sure what to do now. I have to take care of them!"

"What about your condo?"

"That's in a neighborhood district. I think that's the only reason it's standing."

"Mine too," she said.

They all saw what they needed to see.

They parked their cars at WWSI. You could see the uncertainty of what tomorrow would bring was evident.

The elevator doors opened, the view was stirring, but everyone seemed alright. Tom was standing in the conference room looking out over the town.
He felt them come in.

"This is my town; so many need us to stay here to

stay awake to share the truth. Many of the other media papers and stations are covering all this up and justifying it. It's like they want everyone and everything to collapse."

She walked up to him to hug him.

"I do have the answer and the solution, my friend."

"I don't know how that's possible, Laura, but I believe you!"

They all sat at the conference table in Tom's office. Laura began to explain the plan as best she could. Tom never thought it was possible. They talked for what seemed like minutes, but it was hours.

Tom said, "Laura, you have never failed me in all the years we have been together. I trust all you have shared with me.

"How can I help?" Tom was anxious and pacing the floor now. "How can I help to make this happen and have this fight won?"

Tim said, "We are gathering talented people from all over the world. When we have the village of Inspiration orchestrated. When the first production opens...."

Joe continued: "This darkness that we and millions are experiencing will retreat. Its power will be taken from it and then put into its boundaries again."

Tom paced the floor. You could see his mind was one with making this happen. "I can see a way to do this, he shouted!! It has never been done before, but it can be done."

He looked at Tim and Joe--- "once I show you, I know you both will agree. She will too once she experiences it."

"What is it?" They all said together.

"I'll be right back." He returned with a black leather case. Setting it on the table. "This is it."

He slowly opened it up--- Everyone was captivated. "Here is your answer."

He reached inside to bring up a large bifocal type object. A virtual reality headset---

"This little mechanism allows the wearer to experience games and adventures they never thought possible."

Tim and Joe couldn't contain themselves. You would have thought they won the super bowl.

"This is perfect!" Joe yelled out. "It will work. I know it will work."

Tim grabbed Laura and swung her around, "babe, this is it."

The look on Laura's face said it all. "What the hell is it?"

They all laughed, hearing her.

Tom walked over to her and placed them on her

face. "Now, don't move around. Tim, stand beside her.

Now listen to what I am going to say to you. You are going to go to Switzerland and ski down a wonderful slope. Are you ready?"

She nodded.

They all stood beside her, watching her head move around and her hands swinging.

"Oh, my.. oh no-- Holy shit, this is so highhhh," she squealed.

They're holding back the laughter watching her experience this for the first time. She almost fell off the chair, and Tim stopped her.

Tom said, "I am going to turn them off now, Laura, sit still."

She pulled them off her face. Tears flowed down her cheeks.

"Let's do this, she shouted. LET'S DO THIS.!!!

Everyone was jumping around. "Let's do this," they all shouted together. Even Tom jumped around with them.

(All cheered in the council of light! Now they see!!)

Joe was excited, driving back to Brenna's after the meeting with Tom. Everything was coming together perfectly.

When he pulled into the little cabin's driveway, Shadow did his customary greeting. Brenna followed close behind.

"This week seemed like forever!" Brenna said as she hugged him.

His car had a small trailer in tow. It was time to be closer to his love. The little house up the road was still under contract for him to rent.

"What?" She said, "you're going to stay at your house?"

"Yes, I wanted to be a little old fashion here and make sure I don't upset your parents." He laughed.

"Oh, alright," she whined.

It's so good to be home! (He realized this was his home now. He shared what happened in Boston and all he saw.)

"Are Laura and Tim, alright?"

"Oh yeah, they're fine. Tim brought Charlie with him too. We had a long meeting with my boss at the station. He's on board with all of it. He even gave us the best idea. Brenn, it was perfect."

"What?"

"He suggested engaging in virtual reality headsets."

Her eyes brightened---"I know about them. I have used them in Ireland. That's the perfect solution for us.

"I know we were all so excited about the concept. Then we talked about how Tim has sent out emails and messages to arrange for interviews."

"Wow, so much has happened. It's coming along faster than I ever expected."

"We'll need a location to do the interviews. Since we need to be together when they take place. How about the Haven?" Brenna asked.

"Yes, that's large enough. I wanted to try to figure a location, so no one is coming close to our town at first. Especially with what's happening out there. The farther, the better."

"What were you thinking then?"

"Laura's mother's home would be perfect. It's the right distance from Boston and us. It is huge. I went last year for a visit with Laura to see her mom.

"The house is large enough to accommodate all of us. There are two large living room areas that we could open up for offices and conference rooms.

"I haven't asked Laura yet. I will tomorrow and see what her thoughts would be.

"Right now, let's just you and I enjoy being back together. I think she and Tim will have their minds occupied tonight. I don't want to spring too much on them at once."

~*~*~*~

Chapter Seventeen

They all agreed with Laura's mother's home being used in any way that was needed.

"It's perfect," she said to Joe. "What a great idea." Laura's mind was expanding even more with the thought.

"Let me call you right back."

Tim sat at the table in the grand room, watching Laura be Laura.

"Tim," she said with a little teasy whine.

"Oh no-- what are you thinking now? I know that whine."

"Oh, nothing bad, but since we are going to use Mom's house for the interviews and so much chaos is there in Boston. What would you think if??" ...

"Oh, did you want to move into your mother's house?"

"I have a better idea. How about if *We* move into my mother's house? You know my grandmother had a lot to do with us meeting."

He laughed, "so it's her idea, was it?"

"Charlie and Shadow will be best friends and...."

He said, "stop-- You don't have to convince me anymore. But first I have an important call, is that alright?"

"Call? What are you talking about?"

"I'll be back tonight. Let me go check something out. I will be back to take you to dinner."

~*~

Tim dialed Maggie's home, there was no answer; he knew she would be in the café.

His heart raced with excitement. He opened the glove compartment, and the little black box was still there.

In the last year and a half, he was able to get to know this fascinating woman. Fate most assuredly brought their lives together. It was definitely one of the best times in his life. He always felt someday he would find the right woman. It was confirmed with a dream he was given right after he met her.

(*Remembering back: The voice in his dream told him you will meet someone you met while in Spirit. You won't recognize her by name but by the essence of who she is.*

Then, in the desk at my office, remembering the letter was a sign from Laura's grandmother to bring us together. It all makes sense, even to my great grandfather owning the Inn that her family frequented so often. One sign after the next. I remember. And now we are to be together.)

Now to do this the honorable way and ask permission.

As he entered The Journey, there were so many customers. How would he find the right time to talk with Maggie?

She knows you're here, the voice within him said.

Tim hadn't had many experiences like this. He was aware of the possibilities from the trip to Maine. Nothing would surprise him anymore. He waited to see Maggie come through the kitchen door. He felt even more anxious waiting. The door swung open, and there she was with a smile for him, seeing him patiently waiting for her.

"Hello Timothy, what a nice surprise. Would you like some company? Can I get you a cup of coffee or a brew?"

"No, ma'am, I will be back in a short time with Laura. I wanted to talk with you, though, before I bring her here. She is waiting at the Haven for me."

His voice stuttered a bit, trying to find the right words to share with her. "I have learned so much from all of you since meeting Laura. She came into my life so quickly I never expected to be so captivated by what seems like forever ago.

"You all have become my family now. I'm hoping I will be accepted even further than being Laura's boyfriend. I am asking you if I could become her husband. I understand all that she loves and how life with all of you is such an important part of who she is. I want to be a part of that. I am hoping you will give me your blessing to ask her to marry me."

"Come with me, son," and she guided him out to her cottage. He was nervous because he expected her to say yes, of course. But she didn't.

Now was his time to be blended into the family. A family that was unlike any other he had met.

The lights were on as she opened the door. "Come with me."

He followed closely.

A familiar face was standing by the patio door. It was Vivian and his mother. Talise and Nathaniel stood beside them. Nathaniel bowed his head, acknowledging his presence, and Tim remembered him as the angel that appeared to him in his dream. "Hello, Mr. Forget me not," Nathaniel smiled.

Nathaniel continued: "The blessings you receive will be from the ethereal. This union will be one that is admired and a genuine companionship. Brenna and Joseph's life will be in unison with yours. In this marriage, we all are approving and waiting patiently for the words to be exchanged. As well as your children who have been patiently waiting."

"My children?" Timothy's shocked voice said.

"Yes, your children. We chose to do this differently than with Joseph because of your unwavering love. Two little girls and one boy stepped out from behind Vivian.

Their smiles were engraved on his heart. "These are my children?"

"They are cousins-- two will be yours, and one will be Josephs. We wanted you to see them so they will always be in your heart, and nothing will hinder their appearance.

"This vision we are only giving to you. In time you can make Laura aware of this. But for now, no mention of this to her or the others."

He was numb. His heart was racing; he felt light-headed. He hit the floor-----

A voice in the distance was calling to him. "Timothy, Timothy, wake up."

He opened his eyes. Laura was kneeling over him.

Maggie was there too, along with Allura. "Are you alright, son? Should I call an ambulance?"

"No... No, I--- I am fine. Where am I?"

"You're still at the Haven babe with me. You said you had something to do and then all of a sudden you fell to the floor. You seemed so nervous and then fell."

"I'm fine." He looked at Maggie, and she winked.

"Yes, you are fine."

He smiled, knowing she was aware of what took place.

"Let me help you up.".

"I had a dream; I think it was a dream." He slowly stood up, holding his head.

"Dreams are good to have," Maggie commented. "As long as you remember them and don't forget," She stressed the FORGET... "Right, Mr. Forget me not?"

Laura laughed, hearing her say those words.

"I won't forget Maggie, I promise!"

"I think it's best to stay here. We can order in for dinner. You need to rest."

The phone rang: "Is everything alright over there?" -- hearing Brenna's worried voice.

"My goodness, we are a telepathic group, aren't we? Laura laughed. "Yes, Tim decided to take a nose dive to the floor, and no sooner did that happen. Allura and Maggie came storming through the front door."

"Oh my gosh, is he alright?"

"Yes, he seems to be. I am making him take it easy for a few days. I think the stress is catching up to him."

"Now that's a good idea. I think all of us need to do the same. I'll let Joe know he is alright."

~*~

Tim wanted to make his proposal one to remember. He kept racking his brain, trying to come up with a plan. All the things he thought of seemed corny. He wanted it to be genuine from the heart. It had been almost a week, and he felt fine.

He contacted his home office in Boston and knew he would be alright to stay away just a bit longer. His partner was outstanding and had everything under control.

"I have a great idea," he said to Laura. "Since we are going to be making our new home in Marblehead at your mother's home. Let's go there today. I know there's a lot to see from what you have shared. I've driven through there a couple of times on business. If I recall, the bay isn't far at all. I love seeing all the fishing boats out in the water or tied up at the docks."

"This is a great idea, Laura. Let's bring the dogs too. Our little family vacation. How does that sound?"

She jumped into his arms. "I love it, our own little family vacation!

It didn't take them long to pack. Traveling light

these days was their usual from driving back and forth from Boston and Maine.

Laura was excited to go home and see it again. Everything has been so busy since her mom passed. She had only made it there to close the house up. Until she decided what to do with it, now she knew it was to be hers and Tim's home.

Tim did some research on Marblehead, so he was familiar with the area. It was going to be perfect for them to live there. I was less than an hour's drive from Boston. This way, his company wouldn't be affected by his relocating. It was other situations that would interfere, but not his traveling.

He had full intentions to sweep this wonderful woman off her feet, and its planning was relatively easy. He would wait for the perfect time.

As they drove down the quaint narrow streets, you could feel the history that overshadowed the area.

"Look," he pointed to the fishing port with all the boats still attached to the docks. This is a fantastic place. How could I have not come here?

"Did you know the rising of the sun shines here in Marblehead first? That's why on New Year's Day so many gather on the coastline to welcome in the new year."

"I had no idea. That is amazing." Laura smiled, listening to his comments. He was smitten by

Marblehead.

She continued and told him of the lighthouse on the nearby island. "It's light guided ships even back during the Revolutionary war times. This town captivated the colonists because it had so much to offer them.

"I wish they taught this information to more people. Everyone is so much into their now existence they have no idea the historical moments that took place neither here nor even in their towns."

He thought to himself: *This is a beautiful place to raise our family. Then he smiled, remembering his dream.*

Both dogs woke up, sensing it was going to be time to get out of the car. Charlie was half lying on top of Shadow.

Charlie licked Tim's ear.

"Okay, boy, almost there."

~~*

Talise stood beside Vivian. "Are you alright?"
"Yes, I am so pleased they made this decision.
The kids will love it here."
"Yes, they will."
"I know the question will be asked soon."
"Any surprise visitors that you know of"
"We all like surprises now, don't we"

"Welcome home, family," Laura called out as she loosened her seat belt.

Tim was taking in his first view. "Wow, this is nice, babe."

The dogs ran around the yard to stretch from their long ride. They dropped their bags in the foyer and scooted like two children running around the house. The dogs were making themselves at home too.

Laura ran into the kitchen, opening the cupboard her mother always kept the wine. *Thanks, Mom* seeing the cabinet was well stocked. "Let's go out on the patio and relax."

"I'm with ya on that idea." He spun her around like he always did. He loved to hear her giggle.

~*~

The next day they put the plan together. Making the large living room into office spaces for them both to work from home when needed. There was more than enough room in the grandiose house.

Tim called to have the phone lines installed, and their new computers had already arrived. Along with the furniture Tim ordered. Everything was flowing smoothly. They were loving every minute of their blending.

The new phone lines weren't put under any business name. They were being cautious keeping things safe and secure.

The ad was posted on the world wide web. The energy was high for them both.

Both just collapsed on the floor laughing.

"We did it."

~*~*~*~

Chapter Eighteen

December:

Mr. McGrath was overseeing the process at the IV Production location and loved every moment of it. He has a youthful step now, knowing he was part of this fantastic experience.

Cabins were constructed outside the dome for all that would be coming to work on the project. It was incredible to see their little village being created within the hills of Maine.

Brenna began:

"This is wonderful; most of the cabins are completed just in the nick of time before the first snow. Mr. McGrath has been taking care of everything at the building.

"Hiring locals to come to take care of the landscaping and ensure there was help with maintenance and anything unforeseen. It was a dedicated work of patience and love. His service is beyond appreciated.

"The road coming to the building will be secure with

surveillance both in the earthly and ethereal."

They all smiled.

"There are two cabins set back in the property for us. Feel free to bring here what you need, but I am sure you will find other than your personal belongings, everything is here.

"My mother had a large amount of money set in place for the cabins, and of course, you know Tom from WWSI is financially assisting with much of this project.

"Now, we are going to see the actual production of the virtual glasses.

"People that had experience in creating them appeared quickly. Just as we were told, they would."

"Who is here?" Tim wanted to know.

"As we were told before, we will have many that express an interest.

"First, I wanted to ask for help from the ethereal spirit beings who have transitioned and were familiar with their lives to create virtual attire.

"Tomorrow, I will introduce them to you. Then, within a week, others that Laura and Tim have interviewed will come. Remember any uneasy feeling when you meet those of the earthly voice this immediately.

"When we have put into place those needed for the

glasses. In another area of the building will be doing another technique shown to me by my guides. I will share that with you at another time.

"Does anyone have any questions so far?

"Good then, allow me to take you to our fabulous dining area since I am sure you're famished."

"Dining area?" Laura chuckled. "This is like a little village, isn't it?"

"Yes, it is for now, anyway." Brenna smiled.

~*~

The sun shined bright into the windows of the cabins. Joe was the first to wake. He smiled, seeing Brenna resting so peacefully in bed.

The cabins did have everything they needed. He was pleased to discover the coffee pot and coffee. Stepping outside with his cup, he enjoyed the cool breeze.

"Hey, mister early riser." Laura laughed. "Would you like some company? We haven't had a chance to visit since, well, it seems like forever. How are you?"

"I am the happiest I have ever been, Laura. I know there is so much chaos in the world, yet being with Brenna and all of you. It feels like we are all going to be alright.
How about you?"

"I'm fine too. Tim and I are all moved into Mom's house. Who knew just over a year ago we both would be in such unexpected places in our life?"

Joe smiled; "I remember your first meeting with him. He sent you flowers so you wouldn't forget him."

"I remember so many moments, life is filled with surprises lately. Now being a part of this. It tops all of our adventures together for sure."

He agreed. "What will we do with our lives once this is completed, I wonder. That is, will it ever be completed?"

Laura shook her head; "I have no idea. I am sure others do, though." (Again, they laughed.)

Shadow and Charlie appeared, jumping and running around, followed by Tim.

Brenna came out of the cabin, yawning. "What's all the racket out here?"

The foursome plus two sat on the porch just taking in the moment—Ready for what the day was to bring.

~*~

Brenna led them to the dome. As they opened the door, they were greeted by Mr. McGrath. He walked them towards the area that was already arranged to create the glasses.

Three men met them in the middle of the room. You could see they weren't human, but spirit beings.

One spoke: "You have summoned us to assist, and all of us are very pleased. This knowledge we will share was from our

*discoveries within our work in the land of time. Thank you
for asking us to come."*

Brenna approached them as she extended her hand,
knowing that she would be able to touch them since
her clarifying moment with her mother--- "My guides
highly recommended you.

I inquired who would be able to bring this to pass,
and they shared your names."

*"Allow me to introduce myself. I will share who I am and,
of course, my experience. This will allow you to see we, are
most excited to help with what we so loved as we walked the
earth plane so many years ago.*

*"My name is Charles, but my friends call me Charlie. I
was allowed to create by understanding the functioning of
the mind. I was able to change the two-dimensional vision
into three. It took place in the 1800s."*

"Wow," Tim said, and all were amazed.

*"Yes, you heard me say allowed; since all discoveries
aren't new, they always existed, but no one in the realm of
time was aware. Then they say he or she discovered."*

They all were so intent with listening.

*"I created a viewer to look through at images, and thus it
had the appearance of depth. It is quite a lengthy explanation*

yet recognized as a unique experience, one that later would be expanded upon."

Another stepped forward:

"Charlie is correct by his incredible work; my work became possible. I am David--- about eleven years later, I created a lenticular stereoscope with many hours of studying and experimenting.

"What fun it was; we all knew it was just the beginning of seeing things differently. Many tried to duplicate what we were doing; some were successful, some failed.

"The years progressed; we knew that a boy named Morton was coming to the earthly he would be a wonderment in this field. "

Both men patted Morton on the shoulder. Morton humbly smiled.

"My name, yes, is Morton. I was in cinematography as a young lad. During those times, life was difficult, yet I continued in my passion due to my family and their life.

"I created a --- hmm, you would understand it as a cabinet. You would sit in it, and it surrounded you. It was safe; it gave the user an experience such as they had never had before.

"It quickened all their senses, sight, hearing, smell. The chair they sat in even vibrated.

"You can find all of us in your research if you so chose to

do so. Morton laughed; there weren't many named Morton in my field of expertise."

They all laughed and were speechless about what was taking place...

Brenna stepped forward: "These three teachers will be guiding every step of creating the virtual glasses.

"Yes, I know there are many in recent times that have this ability. Yet, I wanted to engage the original creators of this capacity.

"So welcome, Charlie, David, and Morton. We all appreciate you taking part in this. I know you have been with us all along from the first gathering at the Haven. You knew ahead of time you would be asked."

"We will leave you to do what is necessary: Mr. McGrath will make sure all your supplies will be available.

"Remember, the working staff that we have hired is not aware of you and will never be. You are totally in charge. Mr. McGrath will relay any information necessary to Joseph and Timothy to concerns of any kind.

"We have tried to provide helpers that will be of an honest, sincere heart. But as we all are aware. Some will appear that have their agenda.

"There will be a warehouse to safely store your

creations in the rear of the building.

"I would also like to assure you if any workers attempt to take any glasses. As soon as they leave, the production property they will turn to dust in their possession.

"This project is from God and his angels and will not be handled under the same conditions as the earthly."

~*~

They all exited the building in total amazement.

Brenna stared at all of them, waiting for a comment. "Do you have any questions?"

Laura began: "I see they are creating the physical glasses; what will be used to create what is seen as they are worn?"

Brenna answered: "The Village of Inspiration is what will be shared. We will discuss this at a later date. Today I think we all need to make ourselves ready for this to transpire and make our homes and families safe.

"The darkness will be enlivened now that the process has begun. Remember, those against this will try to touch your first layer. You understand what that means."

****

I am of the realm of Spirit: this message comes directly to the one experiencing this book. You need not my name since, in the ethereal, we need not names.

The locations for the "I Believe" experience has begun. As was explained before, this moment was not only taking place in the United States but all over the world.

There are seven continents all will have this available to them. No, not by these four you are reading about, but many others are doing the same thing. Yes, you thought it was just a limited amount would be available.

"I believe" is a worldwide experience to open millions' eyes to take the fear and uncertainty from their hearts.

Within the seven continents, there 249 countries in the earthly realm. You say the United Nations doesn't recognize some. We say that doesn't mean they don't exist.

Structures are at this time coming to pass. They will be placed on Ley lines in the earth plane. Ley lines are lines that crisscross around the globe, latitudinal and longitudinal lines, that are dotted with monuments and natural landforms (such as the great pyramids and Stonehenge.)

They carry along with them rivers of supernatural energy. Along these lines, at the places they intersect, pockets of concentrated energy can be harnessed by certain individuals. There are many skeptics to the validity of the energy that these lines have. I assure you there is more to this realm than man has discovered.

Now let's continue with our foursome and their life's journey.

~*~*~

****

Laura and Tim arrived back in Marblehead to do as they were instructed. Joe and Brenna drove back to Lake Aisling.

(Take care of your families, is what they all kept hearing.)

Laura called Tom and shared with him the progress. He was delighted to hear it was underway.

"Are you alright?" She asked.

"Yes, actually, things have calmed since you were last here. But from the sounds of what you shared. That could change very quickly."

"Yes, it can. I will call you next week. Tom.

"Take care of yourself, okay?"

"Oh, hon, I will, don't you worry about us. Give my best to everyone. I am looking forward to our opening night celebration."

"Me too." She agreed.

~*~

A ray of light shined through her window as if guiding her to the computer. Her fingers flowed across the keys.

These words will be spoken to the assembly as they arrive and are seated:

One of many will be the moderators' voice. It will be different for every presentation.

Time in the earthly is measured by the rising of the sun and the setting. Along with gadgets with quartz stones, clicking on the walls or wrists of many that live by time. In the ethereal, there is no need for time measurements.

The sun is the source of all light to exist as our beloved father is the true source of life. So the light of our father radiates in the realm of spirit. Our loved ones in the ethereal have the light within them and without. Yet you can't measure it in the same latitude as what you experience here in the earthly.

Experiences in spirit just are: they exist and come to pass when the spirit forms call it forth. You see, in the ethereal, nothing is impossible. All your earthly passions can take place in Spirit.

Then why did you come forth?

You needed the contrast; you wanted the contrast. To have and not to have. To experience the opposites of what you had in the ethereal. You have come some of you many times. Always returning home to Spirit. The joy of discovering the joy of having after not having.

Do you see?

When you are touched on the first level with sickness since it does not exist in the ethereal, it is your choice, your decision with the outcome. We don't predetermine it; we only guide you to what it is you want. Sometimes you come and quickly decide it isn't what you expected and ask to return home. So, you do.

Yes, you appear as a small being, but your soul is neither young nor frail. It is the first level, that is.

Now let us share the opportunities you have in the earthly and allow you to know our realms are connected and always have been.

Your earthly body is limited because it is temporal. It will go through different stages as it ages or matures—both within your mind and your body. But your soul is eternal; it never ages. It appears as you want it to be.

Now allow us to begin your experience to BELIEVE.

We are using a village to see more clearly as you view through the glasses you have placed on your eyes. You are also hearing and sensing what we are sharing in a precise moment.

Just watch; then you can interact with any beings that you chose, only by asking. This is only visible and attainable by you and you alone. Remember what you have heard: Think it and create it.

No other will hear your requests nor see what you are seeing.

So, rest back in your seat and enjoy your awakening.

If you chose not to continue, this is your choice too. Just stand and walk towards the back of the room. Our attendants will talk with you or lead you from the building.

Choices in your life have always been yours, just as here. We have made this an age requirement, not for safety, but most children up to 12 still have the memory and knowledge of home untouched. As the years progress and experiences with people and life. There is a tendency to have your thoughts covered and overshadowed with some negative energies, such as anger, doubt, hatred, and judgment.

We will give you a moment… then we shall begin.

Laura re-read what was just given to her. Her keyboard keys just kept being pushed as words were shared with her from her guides and spiritual family.

She took a deep breath, re-reading it.

Let it be so.

Let it be so. She heard a multitude of voices behind her in agreement.

She called for Tim to read it. She was explaining how it happened. He was amazed, so this is how it is?

"Yes, I have never known this so clearly. Everything is coming together.

Chapter Nineteen

December was flying by. Christmas would soon be arriving. The snowstorms in Maine were powerful and ones to be reckoned with. Their contact with Joseph would go down from time to time from frozen phone lines.

Brenna introduced Mr. McGrath to Gladys, the CB lady from Henry's meeting. They both seemed to hit it off pretty well. She knew she would take care of Joseph. It was quite funny for Joe and Brenna to hear of the matchmaking that was taking place.

"I think someone had something to do with this for sure." "Now he has a way to communicate with us too. Gladys will make sure of that."

Snow-covered the land from Lake Aisling to Marblehead and beyond. Mother nature was touching the world of time with all her wonderment. Some enjoyed it, some complained.

Such is in the world of time. Children dressed as quickly as possible to run and play in it while the adults stood by laughing, watching them. Oh, occasionally, some would join in the fun too.

Tim knew the time he would propose to Laura. It was set in his mind. It would be soon.

Both families enjoyed the holiday, decorating and playing in the snow.

Now the year was almost over, and a new year was just around the corner. Tim had everything in place, location, location, location...

A huge festival was being created for the New Years' eve experience at the harbor in Marblehead. The new year's first morning light always reflected on this particular location. For years crowds gathered to bring in the new year with their wishes and hopes for the upcoming year. Old and young shared in the event; it was a tradition.

Tim had it all planned:

"Babe, let's have a nice dinner on the harbor for New Years' night. How about it?"

"That's a perfect idea. It will be our first new years together. I love that idea!"

After talking with a local resident, he made the reservation, which would be the best choice for a late dinner with dancing. The location was near the harbor and was going to be a surprise;

He reserved a room with a balcony view not far from the water's edge. It was surprising he found it at such short notice. (*Then was it, he* thought?) chuckling to himself. This is going to be a moment Laura would always remember. The first of many joyful moments for us.

~~*~

"He's doing it tonight!" Vivian said to Talise.

"I know Nathaniel and I are so excited."

"Mom is coming to," Vivian laughed. "I am sure she will have some extravaganza moment to take place. Mom never allowed a moment to pass without using her magical ways."

~*~

The parking lot was filled with cars as they pulled in. As always, there was a spot not far from the entrance door. Laura glanced at Tim and smiled.

"I know, I get it." He laughed. "Thank you!!" Calling out to the angels.

The music inside was vibrating even out into the parking lot. Tim spun her around and kissed her. It was his trademark with her. It always made her giggle.

"Let's go celebrate our new year and all last year, love."

~*~

The hostess walked them to a table with a blue and white bouquet of forget me not flowers. It was right by the window for a beautiful harbor view.

"Your table, sir."

Laura was so surprised. "It is lovely and --- "

Tim said, "your favorite flowers too."

They both laughed.

The night what timeless. Dancing and laughing, it felt wonderful to relax.

The band leader called out, "Let's everyone stand and welcome in the new year."

The band began playing "Auld Lang Syne' Did you know this song originated in Scotland? He shared with her.

"Really? I didn't know that."

"Aye," he teased in a Scottish brogue voice, my granddad taught me this from a young lad."

Tim pulled Laura closer. "We got this, babe, you and me together."

"Yes, we do!" As they kissed in the new year. Everyone was continuing the party.

Tim said. "I have another surprise for you, my love." He helped her with her coat.

Laura felt as if she was Cinderella; her dreams had come true meeting this wonderful man.

~*~

They walked arm and arm through the brisk winter breeze to their car. But the drive wasn't long, pulling their car into a lovely chalet's driveway.

"We're here."

"What do you mean?"

"We're spending the night here, babe. Not to worry, Joe and Brenna came to the house while we were gone. To take care of the pups."

"Oh my gosh, this is so exciting."

(Of course, they were aware as half the ethereal what would be taking place at sunrise.)

He found the key behind the stone planter and unlocked the door.

As they walked in, the scent of cinnamon filled the little cottage. Candles were lit on the mantle, and white rose peddles made a path toward the master suite.

"Am I dreaming?" She sighed, "I think I dreamt this when I was a little girl."

"May I always be a part of making your dreams come true, Laura."

They didn't get much sleep; the excitement was much too energizing. Tim was ready for the sunrise moment.

He snuggled closer, "come on--- let's catch our first sunrise together."

She turned over sleepy-eyed, letting him lead her to the balcony door.

The snow covered the deck, along with the brisk

winter wind, didn't matter to them. They watched with the doors wide open.

Suddenly shooting stars began to fly across the sky. They both stood in total amazement, watching this spectacular view. Then a glow appeared, but not the sun; it was a magical moment. The night sky lit up with reflections of colored lights all across the sky as far as you could see.

People waiting outside on the shoreline for the first sunrise cheered with joy!

"Tim. I..."

"I had nothing to do with this love."

The ring was already in his hand, waiting for the first crest of light.

"Here it comes!!!!" Everyone shouted.

As they saw the first ray of sunlight, Tim held her from behind and put the ring in front of her eyes.

She started to cry.

"Let's make this forever, Laura Lang, be my wife for forever and a day from this realm to the next."

She turned to him; they kissed through both their tears.

"Yes, Timothy, for forever and a day from this realm to the next."

~*~

The local television stations shared the night's events.

The wonderment of it all crossed across the country. Such a sight would be remembered forever.

~~*~*

The ethereal family cheered.
"Excellent job, Vivian and Judith." Talise complimented them.
They all laughed. "We wanted to create an extravaganza!"
"You most assuredly did."

~~*

Brenna came running out, hearing their car pull into the driveway. The dogs were much quicker, reaching the car. Everyone was jumping around and celebrating.

"Tha mi cho toilichte dhutsa mo phiuthar." Brenna shouted out!

Joe laughed: "you get used to it; she does it when she's feeling excited or mad. You would be able to tell the difference." He chuckled as he shook Tim's hand with congratulations.

They all relaxed together and talked about the previous evening experience. "The sky was beyond belief; Joe and I just got chills watching it.

Now our little foursome is going to be two families. How exciting to begin this year with all this joy."

The snow cleared within a few days, and all drove to see their little village. The mountain roads were still covered with snow, as always melting much slower than the lower land levels.

~*~

It was time for Brenna to share the next process that would be taking place. She called Mr. McGrath the other day and made arrangements for him to meet at the building.

Laura asked: "What's happening today, Brenna?"

Their cars pulled into the Production lot. They were surprised to see other vehicles parked by the cabins.

"It's begun," she said. "The guides and Mr. McGrath have begun creating the glasses needed. Your questions for what else our spirit family has in mind. They will be answered."

Mr. McGrath met them in the entry foyer.

"They all followed Brenna into the grand room. Today we will be talking about Holograms."

"Really?" Joe said. "My uncle did this professionally years ago.

"I know that's why he was brought to Saol. He is an amazing man with many gifts." Joe put his arm around his uncle.

Mr. McGrath began to explain with the knowledge

he had acquired.

~*~

"Japanese researchers created holograms that can be disrupted and moved around by human touch. The touchable holograms, called Fairy Lights, could serve as the beginning to developing technology where humans **could** interact with the hologram."

"Whoa," Laura commented." Fairy lights now that's quite fitting, don't you think?"

They all agreed.

Suddenly a being appeared, walking with a limp around the room. His attire was definitely from the 1900s. He walked around, seeming not to notice them at all. But they most definitely saw him.

"This is Orville Wright; he doesn't see you, but you are familiar with him. Next to him walked a familiar face, Mark Twain. Ah yes, the white hair and confident stature they were both very impressive in their time." Mr. McGrath laughed, enjoying every moment of this.

"Ask a question, Tim. Now when you address him by name, he will come closer to you."

Tim was nervous but excited about this opportunity. "Excuse me, Mr. Wright."

He immediately walked directly across the room to Tim. "Yes, son, how can I be of service?"

"Sir, could you tell me what it was like at the

beginning of your discovery of flight?"

"Well, now that is quite a story, young man; of course, I can't express the trials and successes without talking about Wilber, my brother too.

"We were always intrigued by things that flew from young children, such as toys and the such. I guess you could say it was a passion in us to find a way. But not without some monumental failures. From the beginning, as young lads to when we were aged, it was always on our minds.

"Our father wouldn't allow us to fly together if there was an accident, so both sons wouldn't be lost. One was left to carry on the dream, so to speak. (He snickered)

"When Dad was 82, I took him on his first flight. He knew and trusted us explicitly. In the air, when I took him up. It lasted for seven minutes. He kept shouting, higher, Orville go higher. Of course, I didn't."

(Everyone laughed hearing his story)

"Mr. Wright," Brenna asked, "would you and your brother be available to those here to help if they needed help?"

"Of course, we would, young lady. Of course, our

expertise is in building and airplanes. I mean, we aren't going to teach anyone how to bake a pie or anything."

Again, all laughed. "Thank you, sir, for your precious time."

"Any time, anytime. I know Wilber would love to come help too."

Then he disappeared. Now the only one left was Mark Twain. You could see he was a spry old man. Occasionally taking a jump as he strides along.

They were just enjoying his mannerisms and stature.

"Do you see," Brenna asked. "Can you grasp now what we will be doing?

Angelic beings will appear, but also beings of all statures of life. People that resided in the land of time accomplishing what they chose to. The Spiritual Universe is immersed with guides, helpers and beings anxious to help."

"Mark's talents are many, but one that another author could call on him for his help with their writing."

"Yes, we see," Joe mentioned. "It is so impressive that this will happen for people."

"Mr. McGrath, would you please show us how you did this with the holograms?"

"Of course---

"I use a three-dimensional image formed by the interference of light beams from a laser or other coherent light source.

"Such as a photograph of an interference pattern, which, when suitably illuminated, produces a three-dimensional image.

"This image is created with a laser beam, in which the objects shown look like they
have depth rather than appearing flat and
can seem to move."

"He then held up two photographs—one of Orville Wright and one of Mark Twain."

"How does this coordinate with the blending and the village?" Laura didn't understand.

An angelic guide appeared:

"Mr. McGrath, with others, will be creating a film like attraction to have the viewers see. This will allow them to understand they have the ability to be, do, and accomplish all they would desire in this lifetime. There will be no barriers.

"Remember, you were told these buildings are just buildings. What takes place in them is a precious experience. To make them real "Believers."

"It is then put into our Heavenly fathers' hands to allow them to see angelic beings and beings of all natures outside of their glasses. They will take them off after a time, and then they will experience much of what you have within these four walls in your three visits to learn yourselves."

Everyone was silent.

"Now you have seen the actual production from beginning to completion. I will ask you all to gather your thoughts and be assured it will be an awakening for thousands upon thousands."

All four walked slowly back to their cabins.
No one said a word. Everyone is trying to absorb what just took place.
Laura's phone rang:

"Hey, missy, how's the chilly weather over there?" (It was Maggie.)

"Oh, Maggie, it is so good to hear your voice. We're all safe, and the production is flowing much easier than I expected."

"How would you like some company? Business is slow here, and Allura and I would love to take a road trip.

"We have been talking about it for quite some time. We had a lovely Christmas here with all the bells and whistles. If you know what I mean."

Allura yelled, "more bells than whistles. Tell her, tell her!"

"Tell me what?"

"Oh, your mother and everyone came for a visit and

brought a jolly old gent. You get my drift."

"Santa?!!" Laura yelled out.

"Of course, the one and only sweet girl. He is a jolly one for sure. I think he took a liking to Allura."

"Now stop that Mags; he's married. "

"Have you two been dabbling in the wine there?"

"Wine heck ----We smoked some of that herbal stuff. Santa brought it with him. He makes it special."

"You're kidding with me now, Mags. Santa doesn't smoke pot."

"Huh... you never asked what's in his pipe? Why do you think he is so jolly all the time?"

They all were laughing so hard. Tim had a hard time catching his breath.

"Are you alright to drive this distance?"

"Heck yeah. As long as we don't smoke on the way. (She laughed) What do you think we are one of those crazy old folks that just get in a car and scare the bejesus out of all the other drivers?"

Laura had her on speaker--- Tim couldn't stop laughing, shaking his head yes. Laura put her finger up to shush him.

"We would love to have you come. Then we can show you what is happening here too."

"Alrighty, then it's a road trip date." She shouted to Allura--- "they said yes, Allura!"

They were quite a pair together.

Tim couldn't beat Laura out the front door fast enough to run over to Brenna and Joe's cabin.

"Brenna, Brenna, open up ---if you're not dressed, get dressed!"

Joe opened the door, laughing. "What are you two up to?"

"We have to tell you something; Maggie just called."

They all sat around the warm wood fire and had a good laugh together. A knock at the door pulled their attention away from the moment.

"Compliments from Mr. McGrath and his lady friend," the delivery man said.

It was a gigantic pizza and drinks of all kinds. The note said, we're happy you're here. Now have fun; we will all go into town tomorrow and have breakfast. Gladys and I would like to share some good news.

Everyone settled by the fire at Brenna's and talked about the note. Good news?

"It seems that the angels have created a perfect match." Brenna laughed.

"I think so too. Love is in the air these days." Laura agreed as she cuddled up to Tim.

Now things will be joyful for us. Let's soak it all in and enjoy every moment that comes our way. Experiencing and appreciating joy brings more joy, right?

Right --- they all agreed.

They all seemed to be in a trance staring at the flames in the fire. The crackling sounds allowed them all to be at peace. The dogs cuddled beside each other as they too, seemed mesmerized. This had been a hectic year for them all. "I believe" was coming together and would be touching so many people in the years ahead. Such a funtastic accomplishment, of course, with the assistance of the ethereal realm too.

Chapter Twenty

The snow still covered the roads in the little town. Made the Christmas magic continue. People were window shopping, and you could smell the aroma of the baked goods from the novel café. No matter what was taking place in other parts of the world. This was a place of peace.

~~*

Talise stood beside Nathaniel as they reminisced about their times there when they were in the earthly.

Debra came with Robert and shared in the moment too. It was wonderful to watch their loved ones feeling the same as they did so many years ago. "This is where it all began love," she said.

"Yes, it is."

"We will be having a large celebration with them soon."

"I know, and I am sure you will put some of your exceptional

magic into it too."

"Will we be coming too?" Her grandchildren asked as they stood beside them. "You will be with grandpa and me for now. Soon you will be with your moms and dads."

The tables in the café were filled with hungry customers. Tim noticed a larger table to the side, and there sat Mr. McGrath and Gladys.

Introductions were exchanged. Brenna and Joe were pleased to meet the entertaining Gladys. She extended her hand --- "I left my CB radio home," they all laughed.

"Yes, that was a moment we will never forget." Brenna chuckled.

"Ohhh, that Henry he likes to get me goin."

"Are you ready to order?" The young waitress asked.

Everyone settled in to enjoy their breakfast, knowing Joseph had something special to share with them.

"First, thank you for coming this morning to be with us. I know you're all very busy. Gladys and I only met a few months ago by what I thought was an accident, but I knew better than that. (Brenna laughed, knowing she arranged this through Henry) At our age, it's rare to find a connection with another. She understands I have work to do here. I haven't, nor will I share what is taking place until it is completed."

(Gladys hugged his arm and winked at Brenna: she knew fully aware what was taking place. After all, she was close friends with Henry.)

"When it is completed, she and I would like to commit to each other. We wanted your blessings. Being she will be my wife, I would like to begin our new journey together, sharing the moment that will take place in the project."

Brenna spoke first: "Joseph, you are family. Of course, we give you our blessings."

Everyone cheered, lifting their cups of coffee. Congratulations!!

As they were cheering, the front doorbell chimed as someone entered. It was Mr. Brindle, the town clerk.

"Well, what's goin on in here? It looks like a celebration. I haven't seen this much activity in this café since," ---- he thought for a moment. "I can't think of one."

Everyone laughed.

"Come sit with us, Peter," Gladys took him by the hand. Joseph and I have told the family, we'll be getting married in a few months."

"By god, it's about time. It's tiring watching you two old folks sneaking around. It is quite a gossip story for all of us."

Looking around at all who were seated, he recognized Brenna. "There you be, my sweet Irish friend, did you come back like you said you would, for that license too?"

Joe laughed as he glanced at Brenna. "Yes, sir, I am a man of my word. We would like to get that if your office is opening today?"

Again, laughter filled the café.

Laura tapped Timothy's leg and nudging him. "How about we make that two licenses, sir?"

"I'll be two at once! I have never done that before in this little village. That will be a first."

The foursome said in unison: "first are always special!"

"Let's have a round for everyone," he shouted. "This is a grand day, to be sure."

~*~

Maggie and Allura arrived in Marblehead. This area and all the little towns were very familiar to them both. It felt like a homecoming for them both it had been such a long time since they had been there.

They were told of the wedding plans for both couples that would be taking place at the lighthouse — the perfect location for their beginnings. February chilly with the ocean winds, it was going to be an ideal time knowing tourists would be filling all of New England soon. The Innkeepers at the Bed and Breakfast by the lighthouse were excited to open early for such a wonderful occasion.

~~**~~

Their wedding day

Laura and Brenna stood side by side at the edge of the water. As the waves crested on the rocks, they stood on and below; their gowns flowed in the wind.

It was indeed a magical experience, difficult to put into words. (*Stand beside them as you're reading these words. Feel the wind on your face and celebrate the life-giving energy they both are feeling now.* *)

Above on the upper elevation by the lighthouse, their beloved men are watching, understanding the true essence of the women they love and the life they will be experiencing together.

Behind them are all the family and friends that understand what is going to take place. Every marriage is a blending of families as two lives to find joy in this realm.

Laura and Brenna walked hand in hand upward toward the lighthouse; the lights in the house shined brightly. (They hadn't been lit for years, yet now were glowing.)

Everyone heard a rumble of thunder in the distance, coming closer and closer as they reached the top of the cliff.

It sounded as if a stampede of horses were coming through the sky. Everyone stared in awe as the clouds shifted to reveal an innumerable number of beings standing there with a light surrounding them as the brightest sunlight.

We are here; they all said together.

"This moment is a moment that takes place in all weddings, but most aren't aware." (The minister spoke, fully aware of her job and the moment she was to take part in. Her name? It doesn't matter; the only thing that matters is she knows the blessings that will take place for the celebration.)

"Let us begin."

"Hold hands and never let go."

"Many lessons have been experienced by you all as you have journeyed on your paths. You have paid attention. Taken from life, all that makes you who you are today.

Your passion for life and the things you love have brought you both together. You have followed the many signs as they guided you.

That is how the universe works.

You are all aware of this now.

Like brings like... same brings same. Yet not totally the same. A unique blending of similarities of the most important experiences you both love but differences as well.

All of you have or will at one time be teacher and

student. Teaching and listening...
Many can hear, but the true key is to listen. A teacher
and student do both. Listen to what is taking place that
even words are not necessary to be shared.
How can you tell if the other "listened?"---
Words are only guiding but the trueness of listening is
you SEE it by the expression or action that is taking
place.

Now you can relax--- and go downstream together,
enjoying your journey.
Finding the joy of this life double-fold---
From this moment on, you will see life just as you see it
now. But there will be a slight change of tune
---A new melody.
Since you will now serenade the world with your song
in harmony together.
You are truly blessed in this relationship from this
moment forward."
"May we have the rings please:"
Two women with escorts walked up the path towards
the couples.

One was Brenna's great grandmother: Leah walking
with her husband, Michael.
The other was Laura's grandmother Judith walking

with her husband, Donald.

Leah said: "My precious granddaughter, you came back to find the treasures. You have found them. The treasures were within you. You and Joseph will find more treasures together in this realm. I promise. I hold in my hand two beautiful rings. They come from your great- great grandmother Debra and Robert. They were their circles of love for each other. She placed one ring in Michael's hand, then held hands, keeping the rings in contact with each other.

A circle is the symbol of the sun, the earth, and the universe. It is one of nature's simplest forms.

The rainbow's arc, the halo of the moon, and the smallest of raindrops simulate the circle.

Even when a small stone is cast upon a pond, it generates waves that ever expand circles.

Consider this marriage as being two stones striking the water simultaneously.

The waves interlock and the growth of the blended circles show the combined energies of your life's. Within these rings is the symbol of unity, in which your lives are now joined into one unbroken circle; it is an endless love."

She opened her hand and gave one to Joseph. Then Michael opened his hand and placed it in Brenna's.

"Please place them on each other as your promises are eternal and forever."

They did.

Laura's grandmother stepped forward: Laura had tears flowing down her face. Judith gently wiped her tears and kissed her cheek. Her grandfather had his arm around Timothy's shoulder.

"For thousands of years, lovers have exchanged rings as a token of their vows.

Marriage bands are not of great value themselves. But instead, are made precious by your wearing of them.

It is worn on the third finger, because of an ancient belief that a vein from that finger goes directly to the heart.

In these rings, it is the symbol of unity, in which your lives are now joined in one unbroken circle,

They symbolize that wherever you go, you will always return to one another and to your oneness. May they remind you always of the vows you have taken today and of the promises that have been made."

She took her band off her hand as Donald did the same. "These will bless your union as they did ours." She placed her band in Timothy's hand. Please place it on her finger.

Then Donald placed his band in Laura's hand. He kissed her cheek and nodded. She put the band on Timothy's hand.

The minister spoke:

"Let it be known that you are joined, body and soul in this lifetime and that this bond is sacred and eternal. Your precious double ceremony was a blending of the realms. They always are.

It gives me great pleasure to pronounce that you are now husband and wife."

"You both may now kiss your brides and live happily ever after."

Everyone cheered, knowing this was the beginning of their journey, and it would be quite some time before a gathering of this magnitude took place while they were in the earthly realm.

A lovely sound came from the heavens as if angels singing; it indeed was a magical day for all.

~*~

~*~*~*~

Chapter Twenty-one

April showers bring May flowers. Either way, this year was going to be a month that would be the beginning of many things. A month that would touch our foursome and all that their project was to accomplish.

Yes, it was ready.

The *I Believe* experience would begin on April 25th. Advertising has been created worldwide for the as some called it an "Extravaganza." Billboards from coast to coast with everyone wanting to know what it was about. Their curiosity was sparked. Inquisitive minds worldwide, but the dark energy knew what it was as well as the light.

Those with the gift of intuitiveness were also fully aware. It was time for the world to be on a different level of understanding.

~*~

Laura and Brenna, and their husbands met with the

IV building team creating the virtual glasses.

The three scholars that agreed to assist from the ethereal all stood side by side: Charles, David, and Morton, as well as Mr. McGrath.

"We have completed the process, investigating and using the technology that is available now. It was beyond exceptional for us to see the knowledge that has advanced so much further than the glasses we created. The technology seedling in all of them was from our experiences. We are very pleased.

"Your world is very impressive. We understand why there is such a division from acknowledging the heavenly guides available. They don't realize what they have created came to be from the ethereal. Allowing this to take place."

Mr. McGrath handed everyone a set of glasses. "Here is the finished product:"

"The images that we formulated to appear are seeming to be in animation. What the wearer will see will seem to be very real to them. We know this is just visionary to allow them again to be connected to that which they have forgotten through time."

They placed the glasses on their heads. Then sat in a chair to experience what would be taking place for all who participate.

"First, you are aware of the moderation that will

be spoken before placing the glasses on. Laura, you were given this a while ago."

"Yes, I have it."

"Good, we will have Athena presenting this to the audience. As you know, the buildings that will be used are placed on ley lines, thus allowing the energy to be even more dynamic.
Are you aware?"

"Yes, we are."

"Good."

Tears flowed down their cheeks as they watched and listening to the presentation.

"This is beautiful; it's as if you're taking them into the heavenly realm to experience it."

"Yes, we are."

A bright light appeared,
Four women stood in front of them.

"We will be their guides; each person will be unified with the same vision to begin with. They won't see us. We want them to feel comfortable walking their path unhindered.

Each participant will be able to make their own personal requests, communicating with the angelic realm.

"This is what we in the heavenly have been waiting to take place—the right time and place to answer the questions

of millions upon millions over this planet.

"When loved ones die in their eyes, they are uncertain to what takes place. They are afraid, the village will help them understand. Even though, on a limited basis.

"From their experience will come, assurance, confidence, and peace of mind. They will understand, there is no death. Life continues.

"We have put a memorable sequence in each pair of glasses that will be suited to the wearer. They will be able to soar through the clouds as their loved ones do. They will view their loved ones' life and existence coexisting with the animals and other spirit beings. That is if they chose to.

"Each will have their own personal experience instilled in their souls and take the cloak of uncertainty off from their hearts.

"This is their awakening. After the presentation is completed, everyone will be given a token: golden quartz charm engraved with Believe on it.

We are ready, ladies.

This will begin simultaneously throughout the world. Thunder rolled around the dome with the vibration of all the heavenly beings celebrating

~*~

All countries were participating in the: "I Believe" experience. The locations were strategically placed. After six months, the site would change. It is what the council of light wanted to keep them flowing. Available to as many as could experience the presentation. It was now within their guidance and hands. Those designated would oversee to make the Village of Inspiration moment a life-changing experience.

So much excitement has been taking place, not just for the production finally being available. But Laura and Brenna having now been married for three months shared with their families that they were both pregnant. Everyone was excited since their births would take place in the same month as theirs.

Soft music played as people from all walks of life entered and walked in from the foyer. The seating is as a theater. The rows extend upwards. The ushers guided all to where you felt the most comfortable to be seated. A small white box is handed to all as they sat in their seats.

A moderator's voice thanked everyone for coming. "Please relax and watch our movie. We need to wait until everyone is seated, then you can open the box."

On the stage, there was a movie screen showing beautiful landscapes throughout the world. You felt as if you were flying when you were watching it.

Occasionally some would catch a glimmer of light seeming to fly around the room, then it disappeared, but more would appear. Everyone was very entertained by them.

Within a very short time, the room was filled. You could see elderly couples holding hands and young teenagers. There was no age too old for this, everyone would receive their gift—the gift of awakening.

The lights dimmed; a lovely woman dressed in white came out on the stage. There was a radiance surrounding her that none had ever seen the likes of accept in a dream.

"Good day, my friends,"

Her voice was soft and melancholy.

"My name is Athena. We are so pleased you have found us. Your time here will be filled with many wonderful experiences."

"Experiences that are personal for each of you. Yes, indeed, you have never been in a theater such as this, and I assure you it will touch your heart.

"Time in the earthly is measured by the rising of the sun and the setting. Along with gadgets with quartz stones,

clicking on the walls or wrists of many that live by time. In the ethereal, there is no need for time measurements.

"The sun is the source of all light to exist as our beloved Father is the true source of life. So, the light of our father radiates in the realm of spirit.

"Our loved ones in the ethereal have the light within them and without. Yes, we are referring to your loved ones who have passed. Some of you use the word death.

"Before you walk out the front door, you will have an awakening. An opening of your senses to see, there is nothing to the word death. It doesn't exist, but in man's mind. Life continues; it is never-ending. This, you shall see.

"You see, in the ethereal, nothing is impossible. All your earthly dreams can take place in Spirit.

"Then why did you come forth to the earthly, you ask? You needed the contrast; you wanted to experience the difference.

"To have and not to have. The joy of discovering the joy of having after not having. To experience the opposites of what you had in the ethereal or heavenly.

"You always will in time return home to Spirit or yes if you are more comfortable Heaven.

"At times, some come and quickly decide it isn't what they expected and ask to return home. So, they do.

"Do you see?

"It is always your choice, your decision with the outcome.

We don't predetermine it; we only guide you to what it is you want.

"Yes, you appear as a small being, a baby, but your soul is neither young nor frail.

"It is the first level, that is. What is the first level, you ask? Look at your hands, your arms, your body of flesh and bones. That is the first level; it is temporary. But what is within you is eternal. Your spirit and soul are everlasting.

"Now allow us to begin your experience to BELIEVE.

"Open the boxes on your laps, please. They aren't just glasses, but special glasses. Glasses that will allow you to view a village. Along with so many other things. We are going to take you on a journey of your awakening."

"Don't place them on yet. I wanted to have you see them and understand their use.

"You will also be hearing, seeing, and sensing what we are sharing in a precise moment. The Village of Inspiration will be quite fun for you to experience. You will see.

"Your connection to those within this village are limitless. Where is this village? In your imagination and dreams.

Just watch; as you will be walking through the village. See who appears. Some you may recognize, and others you will only enjoy being with them.

"Some are angelic beings, some spirit beings. Men of

renown are there and great spiritual teachers you have heard of. Yet maybe they passed or you learned from them for a short time, then they transitioned home.

"Here in this moment, you can interact with any beings that you chose, only by asking. This experience is only visible and attainable by you and you alone.

"The best teacher is experience. Now you are being taught by what seems just a pair of glasses. Yet I assure you there is more to this than the glasses. It is your true forever, wakening.

Remember what you have heard:

"No other will hear your requests nor see what you are seeing. The requests take place within, and they are heard. Just as your prayers, take place within and are heard, this is a unique spiritual experience for you.

"So, rest back in your seat and enjoy your awakening. It will begin in a few moments.

"If you chose not to continue, this is your choice too. Just stand and walk towards the back of the room. Our attendants will talk with you or lead you from the building.

"Choices in your life have always been yours, just as here. We have made this an age requirement, not for safety, but most children to the age 12 still have the memory and knowledge from their eternal home untouched.

"As the years' progress and experiences with people and life. There is a tendency to have your thoughts covered and overshadowed with some negative energies, such as anger,

doubt, hatred, and judgment and yes even fear.

"We will give you a moment… then we shall begin.

~*~

She waited examining the reactions of those seated.

A woman stood up; "I sense you are a spiritual guide; may I ask you a question?"

"Of course, my dear."

"Will the sadness that has been happening in the world, our world here be settled?"

The angel smiled: *"There is always going to be sadness in the world my dear. We are here to guide you to the joy.*

The joy you will find within your heart. The joy you will find with direct conversations you may have with your angels *and* guides. *You need not another to mediate for you. As some make you believe. This you will see today.*

Today you will take a shield of protection with you, so you are less aware of the sadness and harm out there. More aware of the blessings you have been given and appreciate them. Do you see?"

The woman had tears in her eyes, "I do see."

"This knowledge you will learn pass on to your children and those you love."

She sat in her seat, holding the glasses in her hands.

"I see everyone has chosen to stay and participate.

"Let's begin:

"Please place the glasses on your head, allowing the

glasses to be directly in front of your eyes."

She watched and guided. *"Now you see a village. Do you see the village?"*

Everyone called "Yes."

"Understand this is a virtual reality experience for you. Begin walking. Walk past the trees, follow the path to the village. Do you see the gazebo in the middle of the park?"

Everyone called "YES."

"Is there a band playing? If not, bring a band to the gazebo just by your thoughts. A band that will play the music you love."

Everyone was ouuuuing and ahhhing as they did this.

The angel smiled, knowing they were on the path.

"Now the village has a variety of shops, apothecaries, country stores; all the businesses you love.

There is a large building coming up on your right. You will see many people standing on the steps. If you would like someone to talk with you about prayer, or anything of your life, call to them and they will come.

You don't have to say anything out loud. This desire is coming from your heart and soul if you want to meet a specific angel or spirit being and receive guidance, call them. Not out loud!!

The movements in their seats showed her they were

doing as she asked.

"Now, I am going to let you experience the village. If you want to fly, you can, yes, without an airplane. If you want to hear the animals and converse with them, you can.

The trees are even alive, sit under them, and they will share their wisdom with you.

This is a limitless experience, enjoy and be at peace."

~*~

The time passed very quickly. You could see everyone was enjoying themselves. Laughter and giggles. Hands flowing through the air, even some stood up as if they were enjoying themselves.

The music began and the lovely woman called out to everyone.

It is time to remove your glasses.

You, though not aware, were on your journey for two hours.

As they did, hologram beings walked toward the stage and lined up on it.

One man called out; "my god is that Benjamin Franklin?"

Another said, "I think that is Moses!"

Oh no, it can't be---

Is that Berle Ives an elderly woman called out?

He smiled and waved to her.

On and on the names were being called out. More and more kept walking to the stage. Angels swooped down and stood in front of the last row of seats.

Everyone was speechless.

Then a bright light appeared on the stage.

Two angelic forms appeared.

"We are so pleased and feel your energy of joy you have just experienced by the Village of Inspiration.

"All of you must realize you have two angels that have accompanied you from the time you entered the earth plane. Have no fear of the world, but enjoy it as much as possible. We...

As he waved his hand to those on the stage with him are here to help you when asked for help.

"If you're a writer, ask for a spirit being in the ethereal to come to assist you with your writing.

"If you are a musician, ask for help. Someone or a few will come, and you will feel their presence surrounding you.

"There are so many here that would love to help and your families who have come home are here too.

"You need not to ask someone to talk with your family. You may do it all by yourself.

The people were all crying from what they experienced and by what they are being shown.

"Signs are given by many in the heavenly realm. They know you have limited abilities things have changed in your way of

communicating.

"But they are still hugging you, and they do sit beside you when you are worried or having fun. They love you to have fun.

"You can ask your angels then be still within, try to still your thoughts from the chatter to hear their words. They will come.

"Some clever beings have discovered a pencil and paper is a good tool to speak with them. Try these.

"We want you to have the veil of doubt lifted. It can happen for you and those you love.

Peace be with you, all my precious ones.

You are so loved and never alone."

They vanished right before their eyes.

Mr. McGrath tapped Joe and Tim on the shoulders as they watched their wives walk out on to the stage:

He whispered, "We couldn't get the hologram to work." They all then knew the Spirit being procession was genuine and smiled.

Brenna and Laura walked hand in hand from the side stage as the beings of light turned into orbs floating around the room. They both smiled, watching and hearing the joy. Timothy and Joseph watched as their lovely wives touched so many with their love.

"Now, I will ask you to please take a deep breath and close your eyes." Brenna guided. "Listen closely to my words. This is an experience you can bring with you whenever you desire. There is more to this life than you have remembered. You are remembering now.

"Thank you, our beloved Father, for guiding us on this journey that only you could bring into being for us all. Be with us, guide us, may we always remember how precious life is.

"Open your eyes please."

"The world of time has, over the years, made you forget.

"Your peace that will soothe your soul and those you love will come from nature.

"Try to step away as much as you can from the world or buildings of concrete. Then the flowing energy of life will calm you when you are stressed or worried.

"Mother nature provides us with tools for your physical and emotional health. Such as stones, plants, and aromatic essences. Keep your eyes open now that they have opened; let no one control you through fear and uncertainty. Please talk with your angels. They will guide you. Life is here, and life in the ethereal, remember this."

"How many of you saw your loved ones?"

Some raised their hands.

"I am so pleased you were confident enough to look for them. They're always by your side. When you transition, the angels will have their hands out to welcome you back home. The love is never-ending, I promise."

"Now open your box on your lap," Laura guided.

"Place the glasses within them and see you have a gift in your box."

All took out a golden quartz charm. Engraved on the charm read: Believe.

"This is yours."

Tom (Laura's boss) was in the audience. He was so pleased with all he saw. He began to applaud everyone joined in.

"We are honored to be with you and look forward to seeing you all again."

Maggie and Allura, along with Joseph and Gladys, were there too. Everyone departed the building; as they did, it became just another shop on the street, blending in with all the quaint shops.

"What the?" They all said together.

Brenna laughed, "as my great grandmother would always say: That was an angel thing."

(Life continues)

Closing words from the angelic realm:

A family reunion took place in the world of Spirit when the last sentence was added to this book. Everyone gathered from the beginning of time to the recently transitioned to discuss the upcoming moments. Their stories have been shared.

The writings you have read, seeming to the reader as sweet stories created and brought to life and your awareness. Many were nonfiction they actually took place and existed.

Their awareness and existence was brought to the writer to share —Each story brings you the readers closer to an understanding that you have forgotten as your time progressed.

This novel, the one you're holding in your hands, brings it all together the alpha and everlasting: the beginning and never-ending story of life.

You have been awakened.
Life goes on and on and on...

We shall see you soon.

The purpose of this author is not to profess or negate any religious guidance that man has available. It is to bring us all together unified as in the ethereal. Our connection to each other is LOVE.

May you all have had a glimmer of the Divine love that surpassed all earthly love and your experiences.

Namaste

DB Lorgan

If you have purchased this book online write to **dblorgan@hotmail.com** with proof of our purchase.

DB Lorgan will have a small gift for you. You will need to assist in the shipping charges for it. That is all;

If you have purchased a signed copy from the author your gift will be sent with the book.

www.ingramcontent.com/pod-product-compliance
Lightning Source LLC
Chambersburg PA
CBHW022156170626
46807CB00005B/2230